ROOKWOOD ASYLUM

Asylum Series Book 1

Written by David Longhorn

ISBN: 9781091617063

Thank You and Bonus Novel!

I'd like to take a moment to thank you for your ongoing support. You make this all possible! To really show you my appreciation for purchasing this book, **I'd love to send you a full-length horror novel in 3 formats (MOBI, EPUB and PDF) absolutely free!**

Download your full-length horror novel, get free short stories, and receive future discounts by visiting www.ScareStreet.com/DavidLonghorn

See you in the shadows,
David Longhorn

PROLOGUE:
1955

Annie heard them coming and tried to make herself small. She was huddled up in the corner of the rubber room. The dark cube stank of disinfectant, sweat, and worse. It stank of fear, misery, hopelessness. Yet it was preferable to what waited for her outside, in the Treatment Room.

"Don't come for me, don't come for me, don't come for me..."

She repeated the invocation, the way she had prayed to God for mercy so often when her ordeal began. She no longer bothered with God, convinced that he had abandoned her as a hopeless sinner, just as her mother said He would. But the habit of praying was hard to break. Although she was seventeen, she still felt like a child.

"Please don't let them take me, not this time..."

Annie kept her voice low, knowing that simply being heard in the corridor by a nurse would be a demerit, mark her out for punishment. The footsteps stopped outside the door of her room. She froze, became utterly silent, too afraid even to breathe. Even now, she crossed her fingers, hoping they would not take her.

Take Big Frank, not me.

She felt ashamed, but Annie still prayed they would take the patient in the room opposite hers. Big Frank screamed and lashed out, kicked and bit. He kept the staff occupied for hours. But deep down she knew this was impossible. Big Frank was 'of limited potential', according to Doctor Palmer. Whereas Annie, she had often heard him say, was 'an extraordinary subject'.

There was a sharp, metallic clang as the bolt was drawn back. Then the door opened, slowly swinging outward. Two white-clad male nurses strode in, and Annie screamed in terror. She knew it was against the rules but could not help it.

"Don't make a fuss, Annie," said one nurse. "You know the drill by now."

She did. She wanted to kick and hit like Big Frank, but could not. She was in restraints, leather manacles fastening together her wrists and ankles. She writhed like a demented caterpillar, trying and failing to bite human flesh, as the nurses picked her up and carried her out of the room like a parcel. Annie continued to scream as she was dropped onto a gurney, strapped down, and wheeled along the corridor. The green-painted walls reminded her of vomit, the dim yellow glow from the light bulbs called to mind the sun she had not seen for months.

Don't think about it, don't think about it, don't think about it...

This was the next stage of the ritual. Annie knew what was coming, but in her despair and confusion, she clung to the belief that one day, the inevitable would not happen. The gurney bumped sharply over the uneven floor tiles, banging her head against the metal frame. She felt a twinge of pain, a trickle of blood. She focused on the injury, the commonplace discomfort. Again, it failed to take her mind off what was to come.

"Here we are," said the lead nurse. "Now, you behave yourself, girl!"

The gurney was pushed through swing doors into the place Annie knew so well. The ECT Room. As she was lifted from the gurney onto a low cot she again tried to fight, but this time a terrible fatalism undermined her. She knew Palmer would do what he liked to her. Annie was his 'best subject'. She had heard the phrase often.

As she was strapped onto the metal cot, memories cascaded through her mind. The terrible pain of giving birth, the brief glimpse of the glistening, bloodied shape of her baby, taken away forever. The man in a suit explaining, in a kindly voice, that she was 'morally depraved', because she was not a married woman. Her first glimpse of Rookwood, the smoke-blackened stone walls, the dull windows. Doctor Palmer was standing in the entrance hall, white-coated, neat, surrounded by his team of subordinate physicians, nurses, orderlies.

No, I won't think about him!

Annie tried to cling to what few moments of happiness she could remember, but it was not easy. Childhood seemed, in her memory, to consist largely of endless hours in a bleak chapel, the minister talking long and loud about sin. The frugal meals, eaten in silence, while her mother berated Annie for her latest sin, real or imaginary. School, where her poverty and shyness left her isolated, had been a lesser ordeal, not a place of joy.

Something happy, I must have been happy once.

But the one moment of kindness she had been shown had been founded on deceit. She saw again the uncle who had given her something called wine at Christmas, the unaccustomed warmth. Then came the fuzziness in her head, the fumbling under the sheets. She felt big, rough hands on her body. And months later had come the thing she had not understood at first, the changes to her body. Adult faces shouting, red with rage, or pale and purse-lipped with a kind of gloating disapproval.

Annie's reverie ended as the doors swung open again. A figure in green medical overalls and a surgical mask stood there, gazing down at her. Doctor Palmer was short, plump, and wore round, wire-rimmed glasses. His expression reminded her of the only teacher she had liked. It was an expression that said, 'I find you interesting, I want to know more about you.' At first, she had dared to hope that Doctor Palmer was on her side, that he would be kind, understanding.

She soon learned the truth.

"Well, well, Annie," said the doctor. "Here we are again."

Palmer nodded to someone out of Annie's field of vision. She was unable to move at all now, her head held rigidly in place, like her body and limbs. But she knew the routine and tried to brace herself for what came next. She still flinched from shock as someone dabbed surgical alcohol onto her arm. Then came the sting of the needle, followed almost at once by the weird, floating sensation. Annie's fears receded, the entire room seemed to fade. Palmer, talking to his assistants about 'scopolamine', was a distant echo.

"There, there, Annie, soon be over."

The round face looked down at her, the mouth under its sparse little mustache turned upward in a smile. Annie knew what came next. Tried to twist her head, escape from the leather, brass-buckled straps across her neck and forehead. It was useless. More alcohol was dabbed onto her, this time onto freshly shaved skin around her temples. A mouth guard was inserted to stop her biting her tongue.

Then she felt the gentle pressure as the electrodes were fixed in place, the instructions given by the harmless-looking doctor. Annie lost all sense of self, all awareness of who or when or where she was.

And then came something totally unexpected. For the first time in months, perhaps for the first time in her life, little Annie Semple was not scared of anything.

***

"Splendid, splendid!"

Doctor Miles Rugeley Palmer felt a familiar exultation, a sense of power and triumph that only came when in total control of a subject. And in this case, the pleasure was all the greater because Annie Semple was his prize guinea pig.

I'll show them all, he thought, as he watched the scopolamine take effect. *All the scoffers, the snobs, the closed minds of the British Psychiatric Association. Crank, am I? We shall see who has the last laugh.*

Annie stopped thrashing and whimpering. For a moment Palmer feared the increased dosage of the drug had knocked the girl out. She was small, underweight, and had been through a lot. Palmer had seen the look in some of his colleagues' eyes; the concern that the girl might actually expire if the experiment continued.

But I'm too close to stop now.

He nodded to his chief assistant and the man placed the electrodes carefully on the sides of the girl's head. Palmer's resentment at those who had mocked or belittled him gave way to pride, an all-embracing pride in his own genius. He imagined himself accepting the Nobel Prize from the King of Sweden, his modest acceptance speech, the chagrin on the faces of his enemies.

And all that stands in my way is the so-called suffering of a worthless girl, some little slut who couldn't keep her knickers on when a man gave her a sip of sherry.

Any doubt about Annie's fitness evaporated. He snapped out a command.

"Twenty-five milliamps, for three seconds."

The operator of the ECT machine looked up, eyes wide. The man's hand hovered over the black dial that regulated amperage. Palmer glared at his subordinate.

"If you want to continue working in the field of medicine," he said slowly, "give her the required amount."

The operator lowered his eyes to the controls, unable to face down Palmer. The man twisted the dial, held it for a count of three. Annie Semple arched her back, insofar as she could within the heavy restraint. Her eyes rolled up into her skull, and a trickle of drool appeared at the corner of her mouth. Then the count of three was up, and the slender body slumped, inert under her stained cotton gown.

"Bring her round!" Palmer barked.

A nurse sprang forward, began slapping the girl's pale cheeks. Annie recovered consciousness, looked around her in puzzlement. Then Palmer saw recognition dawn on the delicate features.

"Don't worry, my dear," he said. "We will soon be making history, the two of us."

Palmer was already contemplating the next session in the Experiment Room. He confidently expected Annie would provide the best evidence of her powers yet. He had been documenting her extraordinary abilities for nearly three months now and had hours of film footage. That, added to sworn statements from his compliant staff, should be enough.

But it might not be, he thought, as the girl was unstrapped and lifted onto the gurney again. *I might need to go further, stimulate her strange talents even more.*

As the nurses were about to secure Annie to the gurney the girl began to jerk and flail her limbs. Impatient, Palmer stepped forward and grabbed one thin arm, held her down until she was secured. When he let go he noticed the red bruises left by his fingers and thumb.

Just the sort of thing do-gooders would condemn as 'inhumane'. Such people never grasp the big picture.

He made a mental note to make sure the film camera was aimed at Annie from the other side so the marks would not show.

"Come on!" he snapped. "We need to get the tests underway before the drug leaves her system."

The nurses began to wheel the gurney towards the swing doors of the ECT room. But suddenly the gurney swerved, struck Palmer a painful blow on the thigh. Cursing, the doctor reeled back, colliding with a tray of instruments, knocking several onto the floor.

"Sorry, chief," said one nurse. "This bloody thing has a mind of its own."

Palmer was about to lambast the man for his idiocy when he felt the words dry on his lips. His collision with the wheeled instrument tray had spilled, among other things, a pair of surgical scissors onto the floor. The scissors were not lying where they had fallen, though. Instead, they were standing up on their points, the finger-loops slowly turning like absurd owl eyes.

"What the hell?"

The ECT operator was looking around him, eyes rolling with alarm. Now Palmer could feel it, too, the vibration that seemed to be passing through the floor, the walls, rattling fixtures, causing a loose tile to fall off a wall with an alarming crash.

"It's an earthquake!" exclaimed the operator.

"We don't get earthquakes in England, you moron!" Palmer retorted. "It's probably subsidence—this whole area is riddled with old coal workings."

But even as he said the words Palmer doubted his rationalization. And then he saw something that proved him wrong. The buckles that held Annie Semple down on her gurney were slowly being unfastened. As soon as the nurses saw it, they backed off, one tripping over the cot, falling onto his backside.

"Don't panic, you fools!" Palmer shouted. "Don't let her get up!"

But the girl was already free, the thick leather straps flung back, the thin form sitting up. The nurse who was still standing lurched forward, meaty arms outstretched. A hefty brown bottle flew off a shelf and struck the man on the side of the head. Glass shattered, iodine splashed wildly across the room, and the nurse went down heavily. Palmer gawped, struggling to grasp what had just happened. The brown puddle of iodine was turning red.

"Sorry, Doctor Palmer," said Annie. "I don't think you'll be getting your Nobel Prize."

"Annie?" he replied, backing towards the doorway. "Annie, behave yourself."

This can't be happening, he thought. *She does not have this kind of power. She struggles to move a matchstick sometimes!*

The bonds that restrained Annie's legs flew open. She swung them over the side of the gurney and stood up. Then she staggered, fell against the ECT machine, held herself up by one emaciated arm.

"You need to lie down," Palmer began, struggling to preserve his authoritative tone. "You must not over-exert—"

A second bottle flew from the shelf, then a third. The nurse who had retreated to the doorway ducked, and the missiles shattered against the swing doors. Then the nurse was gone, leaving his colleague lying unconscious. Annie looked at the man who had put the voltage through her head and gave a little smile.

"You hurt me so much," she said quietly, almost inaudible over the continuing vibration. "But you finally burned out something useful. Quite by chance, you took away my fear."

A metal tray flew up into the air, rotated swiftly, then scythed across the room at phenomenal speed. It knocked the ECT operator off his feet. Stunned, he sprawled in a corner, vainly trying to ward off the attack. The metal tray descended, striking vicious blows that audibly cracked the man's fingers. Then it struck him in the face repeatedly, pummeling his nose to a bloody mess.

While the onslaught was maiming his subordinate, Palmer had been edging towards the doors. But just as he was about to make a dash for it, Annie's bloodshot eyes turned to him again.

"No, Doctor Palmer," she said. "You told him to do it. You told them all how to hurt me. Now, I'm free from fear. I can finally give you all the results you wanted. And more."

"Annie!" Palmer pleaded, his self-control all but gone. "Don't do something you'll regret!"

Annie grinned at that.

"Oh, I won't regret it at all."

Palmer lunged for the doorway, but invisible hands grabbed him, held him in place, one foot off the ground. Then he was turned in the air, half-dragged, half-carried over to the metal cot. He knew what was coming. He would be strapped down, subject to who-knew-what deranged form of torture. But then he felt the grip on his body slacken, and he fell to his knees.

Palmer looked up at his tormentor. A trickle of blood was running from Annie's left nostril.

Brain aneurism, Palmer guessed, still a clinician despite his terror. *She's massively overstraining her mind. If I can just hold out—*

"Annie!" he pleaded, trying to sound compassionate, friendly. "Annie, you're not well."

The girl laughed at that, throwing her head back, then coughed as blood ran into her mouth.

"Oh, I know that, Doctor," she managed to say, wiping her nose with the back of her hand. "But you made me this way. You made all of us the way we are, all your guinea pigs. Like animals in a zoo, all in cages."

Her expression changed, and again blood oozed from her nose. Palmer braced himself for an attack, lifting his arms to cover his head. But nothing flew across the room. Instead, Palmer heard shouts, clanging noises, running footsteps. Annie's eyes seemed unfocused. He took his chance and ran out into the corridor.

At first, Palmer thought the general air of confusion was because staff were rushing to help him control Annie. But then he saw that they were running in all directions, their shouts of panic echoing in the corridors. A young doctor almost ran into him, trying to dodge around the senior clinician. Palmer grabbed the man by his shoulders, shouted into his face.

"What's happening, man?" he demanded. "Get a grip—I need help with the Semple girl!"

"They're all free!" the young doctor shouted and wriggled free of Palmer's grip, fleeing.

It took a moment for the meaning to sink in. Then Palmer saw two male nurses grappling with the patient they called Big Frank. As the doctor watched, Big Frank casually hurled one of his antagonists against a wall. The nurse slid down to the floor, leaving a dark smear on the paintwork. The other nurse tried to disengage from the struggle, but Big Frank snapped the man's neck, all the while smiling beatifically. Then the maniac looked up and saw Palmer.

"Looks like you can't go that way," said Annie.

Palmer spun round to see the girl moving towards him. Two trickles of blood were now flowing down from her nose. Her eyes had no whites, thanks to burst capillaries. Yet her power was still so potent that her bare feet were hanging a few inches above the floor. She was floating toward him.

So much power, Palmer thought, his scientific curiosity still able to function. *It must be burning her out. She can't have much longer.*

"Long enough," retorted Annie.

There was a distant boom, more screams, more panicky shouting. Palmer thought of the compressed gas cylinders, oxygen and ether. If someone had started a fire, the entire hospital could be destroyed.

"Don't worry," Annie said, her voice strained. "We still have enough time."

Two huge arms grasped Palmer from behind, lifted him off his feet. Big Frank's foul breath assailed the doctor as he writhed, his huge captor giggling. Annie floated back toward the ECT Room. A doctor ran around the corner and stopped at the bizarre sight.

"Help me, man!" gasped Palmer, struggling against the crushing pressure of Frank's huge arms.

The doctor hesitated for a moment. Annie did not seem to acknowledge the man's existence, but suddenly his stethoscope flew up and wound itself around his neck. The rubber hose knotted itself, pulled tight. As Frank shoved Palmer through the double doors, the doctor writhed on the ground, clutching desperately at the stethoscope.

"Doctors—are supposed—to help people," Annie said, her voice a painful croak.

Even in the grip of the hefty lunatic, Palmer clutched at the hope that Annie might simply die, or at least lose consciousness. He knew that the release of all his other subjects would be hard to deal with, even harder to explain. But with the girl out of action, Palmer might at least have a chance.

"No," Annie said. "No hope for you, doctor."

Frank lifted Palmer and dropped him roughly onto the metal cot. The leather restraints whipped around like striking cobras and buckled themselves. Then Palmer felt the moistened pads of the electrodes clamp themselves to the sides of his head.

"Frank," said Annie, sounding even weaker now. "Turn it up. Turn it up all the way."

The big man lumbered around the cot, then gawped at the controls of the ECT machine. The hesitation gave fresh hope to Palmer.

"Frank," he said, trying to sound firm. "Frank, you don't have to do this. You'll get into trouble. If you let me go, I can—"

Agonizing pain shot through him. The last thing Palmer, as a living man, saw was Annie, sinking gradually to the floor, a huge patch of dark blood almost covering the front of her hospital gown.

And then he was in Hell.

***

"Come on, Fatso, get moving!"

Owen made a muffled protest at the use of his hated nickname, then began straining extra hard to clamber over the wall. It was not a high wall, and the others had had no problem with it. Eventually, Owen managed it, falling into the undergrowth with a squeak of dismay. When he got back on his feet, he joined the rest of the gang for what their leader called 'the debriefing'.

"Okay," said Tommo, "this place burned down four months back because the loonies got out and murdered the doctors and nurses, then set the place on fire. That's fact, right?"

Tommo looked around the little group, faces illuminated by the weak, yellow light of his flashlight. He lifted the light, shone it full in the face of Micky, the would-be recruit.

"People say it's haunted, the whole East Wing," Tommo went on, in a low, menacing voice. "They say that anybody who goes in there might meet the ghosts of homicidal maniacs."

Micky, an undersized boy of twelve, gulped but said nothing. Fatso and Bill, the other two members of the Black Hand Gang, sniggered and nudged each other. Tommo shushed them, turned the beam on Micky again.

"If you want to join the Black Hand," he said, "you've got to spend half an hour in there. We've all done it, haven't we lads?"

Owen breathed in sharply.

That wasn't the plan, he thought.

"Haven't we, lads?" Tommo repeated, with heavy emphasis.

"Yeah, definitely!" piped up Bill, the loyal follower. A moment later, Fatso chimed in with a mumbled noise that he tried to make sound affirmative.

"So, Micky," Tommo continued, "all you have to do is go in there, find something to bring out—like a document or a surgeon's mask, that kind of thing—and then come back. You've got thirty minutes."

Tommo looked ostentatiously at his wristwatch.

"Starting now, Micky."

The smaller boy hesitated, but only for a moment. Then he set off through the overgrown grass toward the East Wing. It was a full moon, and when Tommo clicked off his flashlight, Owen could still see Micky. The boy's dwindling figure looked very small against the half-wrecked building.

"Why'd you do that, Tommo?" Owen asked. "We never went in there. I thought we just came here to scare him a bit? Nobody goes in there at night!"

Tommo's voice dripped with contempt when he replied.

"Because, Fatso, Micky smells of piss," he said. "He's wet, outside and in. Always hanging around, he's so desperate to be in with somebody. We don't want his sort in the Black Hand. But we have to give him a test, don't we? It's in the rules. And when he fails his test, we'll have a good laugh."

Bill guffawed.

"Yeah, when he comes running back like a toddler, it'll be great. You're brilliant, Tommo!"

"Very true," Tommo replied, preeningly.

Owen remained silent as the other two began to speculate on how long Micky would last out. Tommo suggested ten minutes, Bill guessed no more than five. But five minutes passed without any sign of Micky, then ten went by and the boy still did not reappear. When half an hour had passed, Owen broke the silence to wonder if Micky might have hurt himself, maybe had a fall.

"That building is structurally unsafe, my dad says," he added.

"Oh, shut up, Fatso," Tommo retorted, and seemed about to heap more abuse on Owen, but at that moment, Bill pointed at the dark bulk of the East Wing.

"See! He's coming back!"

Sure enough, Owen could just make out someone picking their way past heaps of rubble. Tommo flicked on his torch for a second, just long enough to show their position. Showing a light for too long in Rookwood's grounds would alert the caretaker, maybe even the police. Micky came straight to them, though, and then stood facing the three Black Hand members.

"You're back, then," said Tommo, his voice surly. "Half an hour. Well done."

"I met a girl," said Micky, his voice oddly flat, expressionless. "She told me you were being cruel. That you'd never let me in the gang. You just wanted to scare me."

"Balls!" sneered Tommo. "Like any girl would talk to you. And what would a girl be doing in there, anyway?"

"Maybe she's a ghost!" jeered Bill.

Nobody laughed at that. There was a long pause before Micky spoke again.

"Then I met all the other people," he said, as if he had not even heard Tommo's taunts. "They said you were bad, Tommo. That you'd hurt me if you could."

"You're talking bollocks!" Tommo said, sounding angry now, and a little bit scared. "You want me to give you a smack in the gob?"

Owen suddenly wished that he could see Micky more clearly in the moonlight. The smaller boy seemed to have one hand behind his back. Owen stepped back a pace as Tommo flicked on his flashlight again, shone it into Micky's face. The boy's eyes were wide, seemingly glazed over. What was stranger, he did not blink.

Like he's walking in his sleep, Owen thought. *I don't like this.*

"Something's wrong," he said aloud, and backed off some more. "He doesn't seem right, Tommo."

As soon as he said it, he realized that Tommo would take the warning as a challenge. The gang leader stepped forward, jabbed a finger into Micky's chest.

"Anyway," Tommo said, loudly. "Just because you spent half an hour in there with your imaginary girlfriend, that doesn't mean you get to join our gang. Remember I said you had to bring something out? Proof you didn't just dodge around the corner and hide *outside* the East Wing."

"I brought something," Micky replied, bringing his hand out from behind his back. "This do you, lad?"

Something glinted brightly in the torchlight, and then Tommo was staggering backward, making a gurgling sound. Bill screamed, high-pitched and terrified. Owen did not want to see what was happening, and instead ran back towards the perimeter wall. The beam of the flashlight cast shadows as he ran, not just Owen's hefty form, but also two others. One was a small silhouette, making a slashing motion with one hand. The other was holding up its hands in front of its face. Owen heard Bill scream again, and start to sob.

I can do it, Owen thought. *I can get over. I got in, I can get out.*

He began to try and scale the wall, hands and feet scrabbling desperately for holds in the weathered brickwork. Behind him, the torch went out.

CHAPTER 1

"Poor Mister Fluffykins," remarked Paul Mahan, taking off his glasses to examine the home-made poster. "I wonder if they ever found him?"

Kate Bewick looked puzzled. Paul gestured at the trunk of a tree, one of the dozen or so ancient oaks that lined Blaydon Avenue. Kate examined the faded rectangle with its portrait of a long-haired white cat, then smiled. Her professional demeanor had been ruffled for a moment.

"Ah, yes," she said, briskly. "Lost cat. People around here certainly do love their pets! But, of course, it's a very nice area, good mix of professional people, retirees, some young families—but not too many children! No hordes of youngsters thundering up and down the stairs."

She moved on, striding quickly up to the impressive, cast-iron gates of Rookwood Apartments. Kate punched in a code on a panel on the right-hand gatepost. Nothing seemed to happen. Paul, losing interest in the faded 'Lost Cat' poster, went to stand by the woman.

"Sorry!" she said, again sounding slightly ruffled. "Minor technical glitch. I'll just ask the caretaker to let us in."

Kate began to push a buzzer on the metal panel. There was no response, and while they waited, Paul looked through the gates at the building. He had seen online pictures but knew how easily they were manipulated. However, from this admittedly limited perspective, Rookwood looked impressive.

The building had been constructed from light-colored sandstone in the early twentieth century. It consisted of a central block of three floors, with two wings attached. The main block and the West Wing had been thoroughly refurbished. The East Wing, however, was still a work in progress. The latter was apparent from scaffolding and sheets of green plastic covering much of the structure.

"Hello? Declan?" Kate called into the grille.

Again, Paul noticed that she sounded slightly more stressed than might be expected from such a minor hitch. Kate Bewick struck him as a woman permanently wound-up, perhaps a little too close to breaking point.

But then, look at me, he thought. *I'm only looking at this place because my old life fell apart.*

A small voice crackled from the speaker grille, then there was a click and the barely audible hum of electric motors. The gates opened, swinging back silently, reminding Paul of old horror movies. Kate gestured Paul to go through. He walked inside the bounds of Rookwood, feet crunching on the gravel driveway. Kate got back into her Nissan and drove inside. The gates closed behind the car as Paul got in.

"How many people have already moved in?" he asked as the little car swept up the curving drive. "I read there were maybe a dozen?"

"About that," Kate said breezily. "We plan to have seventy apartments in total, but only forty-four are ready now."

Paul nodded, peering up at the impressive façade of the building. He felt its rows of tall, narrow windows gave Rookwood a watchful air.

As if the place is on the lookout for trouble. Or victims.

"Isn't it usual to finish the work before you start renting out flats?" he asked.

"Oh, yes," replied Kate, as she stopped the car. "But we felt that—as there were so many inquiries from prospective tenants—we should let the finished apartments while we added the finishing touches."

As he got out of the Nissan a second time Paul heard a high-pitched, mechanical whine start up from somewhere in the East Wing.

"Some fairly major touches being added there," he said, half-jokingly. "Is there any problem with noise? Power tools can be rather irritating."

Kate was insistent that the apartments were all double-glazed to muffle outside noise. He shouldn't hear anything from as far away as the East Wing. She ushered him into the well-lit, ultra-modern foyer, where they were greeted by a tall, rangy man with a bald head and a fiery-red hipster beard.

"This is Declan Mooney!" Kate said. "He's our caretaker and general handyman. Declan, this is Doctor Mahan, a lecturer at the university."

"Ah, you're the American gent," said Declan. "Pleased to meet you."

"And you," Paul replied. "And I've been over here so long my folks claim they can hear a touch of British in my accent—though maybe they're joking."

Paul recognized the man's accent as Northern Irish. As they shook hands, he noticed an elaborate tattoo on Declan's wrist. It seemed to be a Celtic knot of some kind. On the back of his right hand, Paul noticed, there was a bare patch where, he assumed, a smaller tat had been removed.

"Declan is a treasure," Kate went on. "Always busy with some little job or other."

"Gates buggered again?" the caretaker asked her. "Best just leave them open until the contractor gets off his arse and fixes them."

They commenced an involved discussion concerning an automatic opening system that, Paul gathered, supposedly allowed residents to drive in without getting out of their cars. Unfortunately, the system had never worked properly. Declan was of the opinion that this was down to 'dodgy electrics' that needed to be 'looked at'. Kate, with a sidelong glance at Paul, tried to laugh off the suggestion. Eventually, the caretaker shrugged and grinned.

"Ah, I daresay it's just more of those teething troubles, Kate," he said. "I'll let you get on now. Nice meeting you, Paul!"

There was a pair of elevators, one of which was labeled OUT OF ORDER. Paul decided not to ask about the sign, and Kate volunteered no information. But as they ascended in the lift that did work, he could not help asking about Rookwood's history.

"Sorry," he added, "I bet everyone goes on about it."

"Oh, everybody does," Kate said, looking relieved. "I don't mind talking about it. Some people say the building's haunted. Things have been heard and seen, they say. But I suspect that's just imagination. I've been manager here for nearly four months, and the closest I've come—"

The lights went out, and the elevator lurched to a stop. Paul tottered, reached out instinctively for the rail, and felt Kate grabbing his other arm. For a long moment they were in darkness, standing close together, neither speaking. Then the lights flickered on again, and Paul felt the metal box begin to rise.

"Whoops!" said Kate, letting go of Paul. "Sorry about that, another one of our gremlins in the works, I'm afraid."

Paul did not reply at first, instead wondering how many other 'gremlins' might be lurking in the fabric of the building.

"I guess," he said, as shiny doors slid open in front of them. "We can take the stairs on the way down. I could do with the exercise."

Paul emerged from the elevator into a pool of multi-colored light. They were at the end of a long hallway by a stained-glass window, about six feet high and half as wide. Paul stopped to study it, guessed that it was from the art nouveau period that pre-dated the First World War.

"Ah, yes," said Kate, "one of our little treasures. A dozen or so windows were specially commissioned by the city for the original building."

"The asylum, you mean?" asked Paul.

"Yes, the asylum. It's one of only three windows that survived the fire back in 1955. The others cracked in the heat, apparently."

Paul looked at the window more closely. It showed a white-robed woman, evidently a saint by her halo, standing in the midst of a crowd. Ornate scrollwork at the bottom of the window bore Gothic lettering. It took Paul a moment to decipher it.

"Saint Dymphna ministering to lunatics," he read. "Wow, they were kind of on the nose about mental illness in the old days."

"Quite," said Kate briskly. "We live in more enlightened times. Now, if you'd care to follow me along, I'll show you the apartment."

***

An American, thought Declan Mooney, as he watched the elevator doors close. *Seems ordinary enough. But you never know.*

He ran the fingers of his left hand over the patch of skin where he had had the tattoo removed. That had been nearly ten years ago, but he could still see the slogan, the flag. It had not been illegal, strictly speaking. But it had guaranteed that nobody meeting him could have doubted his allegiance, his origins. In the right area, it was a safe conduct pass. But if he had simply walked into the wrong pub, asked the wrong guy for directions, the tattoo could have earned him a beating. Or worse.

As if getting a bloody picture taken off my skin could solve the problem.

Declan tried to shrug off unpleasant thoughts as he made his way back to the modern office he disliked. He would have preferred a dark little cubbyhole somewhere, or a shed in the grounds. But Kate had been insistent on his membership to 'the core team' and wanted him close at hand.

Not a bad lass, he thought. *And a fine pair of legs on her. But naïve. Not the sort of person to be running a place like this.*

Declan sat down at his desk, turned on his company-issued computer, and began to log the day's repairs, complaints, and faults. The log on Rookwood's intranet was fuller than any he had kept in the past when he had worked in Liverpool and Manchester. The building clearly had more teething troubles than average, and it was not even finished.

The East Wing, he thought. *Hanging over us all in its way.*

He closed the online log and got up, stretched. He felt a slight twinge of pain in his neck, rubbed the area for a few moments. Then he set off on his rounds, his daily routine of checking lights and common spaces, making sure nothing else had failed for no readily apparent reason.

Gremlins, she calls them, he thought. *Makes the unknown seem all cuddly, small, and trivial. But maybe it isn't.*

As he passed through the foyer, he thought he glimpsed someone from the corner of his eye. When he stopped to look out at the sunlit driveway, he saw no one. He continued on his way but could not shake the notion that he had caught someone watching him. And he felt the odd, crawling sensation up his spine as he went along an empty corridor. More than once he glanced over his shoulder, but of course, he was not being followed. He attributed the creepy sensation to the lights, which were triggered by motion sensors. They created moving pools of radiance. A few yards ahead of him and behind, the corridor was dim, with more shadows than he cared for.

Sure, and how would they track me down here anyway? Declan asked himself. *You're just being bloody paranoid, man. It's not like you were ever a big boss in the organization. Nah, you were just a daft lad who took messages, kept watch on the corner. Nothing too heinous at all. Thousands did worse and got away with worse.*

"You hid those rifles in your ma's attic."

The words were spoken directly into his ear, the voice an urgent whisper. Declan spun around, anger rising, fists raised. But there was no one to lash out at or defend against. He was still alone in the silent, carpeted corridor.

"I'm hearing things," he said aloud.

He had stood still for just long enough for the lights to go out. Declan waved an arm to trigger the sensors. In the split-second before the light was restored, he thought he saw a figure at the far end of the corridor. It was masked, wearing a black beret, its clothes baggy combats, heavy boots. One arm hung by its side, and in its hand, he saw the sharp outline of a gun, an automatic pistol.

"Nobody there!" he insisted as the ominous silhouette vanished.

"Mind playing tricks."

The sound of a drill pierced the air, a noise that would normally be mildly irritating. But now it was a relief, a reminder of the mundane world of work, of practical matters and practical men. Declan turned and walked on, taking his moving pool of light with him, heading for the East Wing.

I'll just have a little chat with those builder lads, he told himself. *See how they're getting on. It's not good to be alone too much around here.*

***

The apartment itself was impressive, living up to the pictures and fulsome words on the company website. Paul found himself making approving noises as Kate showed him around, sensed the manager relaxing a little as she picked up on his reactions.

"It's the first place I've seen so far that I can actually imagine living in," he admitted to her. "At least, living like a human being. Everything else in my price range is kind of bleak, in terms of location, and space."

"Yes," Kate said, "the rental market in the area is somewhat patchy. This is one of the most competitive developments in the Tynecastle area."

Paul checked the small kitchen, then the bathroom. The flat was exactly as advertised. He took off his glasses, rubbed the bridge of his nose. It was a mannerism he had cultivated to buy time when a student asked him a tricky question, or a very stupid one. Now, he was using the brief pause to decide whether to ask an obvious question of his own.

"Okay," he said finally. "Why is the rent so low? For a brand-new apartment in a state-of-the-art building?"

Kate Bewick's smile did not falter.

"We had some bad PR because of the whole asylum thing," she admitted. "So we dropped the price a little, to get people in quickly, and scotch the—well, silly rumors."

Paul was about to ask for details about the rumors when a stocky, gray-haired woman appeared in the apartment doorway. Kate, with a hint of relief, introduced the newcomer as 'Mrs. Prescott, chair of the Tenants Association'. After some minor chit-chat, Mrs. Prescott started talking about problems with the building. Kate's smile froze on her face.

"We have a lift that's been out of order for nearly a month now," Mrs. Prescott pointed out. "And there are still major problems with the electrical system in general."

"Oh?" Paul asked. "Tell me more."

"Power surges," replied Mrs. Prescott. "Strong enough to blow fuses in several apartments. My own hairdryer nearly exploded the other day."

"Let's talk about this outside, Sadie," Kate put in, taking the woman lightly by the elbow. "Paul, why not just wait here and get the feel of the place—take a look at the view, it's quite impressive."

Paul heard Sadie Prescott continue to list gripes as the two women receded along the corridor. Smiling to himself, he wondered if he could risk moving into a place that seemed to have so many teething problems. He went to the large picture window and looked out. The view was impressive, he had to concede. Rookwood stood on a low hill in the northern suburbs of Tynecastle. The ancient English city spread out below it, looking its best in the morning sunlight. He could make out the cathedral, the graceful arch of the road bridge, tower blocks in the business district. He tried to orient himself, find the university, perhaps even his own building.

"Hello."

It was a low, hesitant voice. Paul turned to see a petite young woman standing in the doorway. She was about five foot three, pale, with dark hair and eyes. She was wearing a shapeless, dark gray dress that nearly reached her knees, and black, low-heeled shoes. Paul guessed her age as late teens, no more than early twenties. Her face was a little too round, her mouth too thin, to be considered beautiful. But she was pretty, and he felt himself responding to her shy smile.

"Hi!" he said. "You live here, I guess?"

***

Sammy had his ear protectors on, so he could not hear Pavel shouting at him. But he could tell from the foreman's expression that he was in trouble again. Sammy turned off the drill, withdrew the bit from the stonework. He could see Pavel mouthing words, the foreman's face flushed with anger.

Jesus Christ, Sammy thought. *What have I done now? I hit the mark he chalked there with his own hand, but he's still pissed off at me.*

Sammy removed his ear protectors and heard exactly why Pavel was upset.

"You used the wrong bit!" the Pole shouted. "The hole is too big now!"

Sammy looked down dumbly at the drill bit. Then he looked at the hole where Pavel's chalked X had vanished. Next to it was a number. Sammy had assumed it was the number of the hole, one of dozens to be drilled in the walls of the old building. But no. Now he looked at it more closely, he could see it was a gauge in millimeters. And he, Sammy, had used the wrong size.

"Oh," he said, feeling immensely stupid. "Sorry boss."

Pavel seemed to lose the power of speech. Sammy felt an irrational surge of anger, looking round at the other men. They were all careful not to meet his gaze, looking embarrassed for him. All except for Doug, the joker in the pack. Doug was smirking to himself. Doug had sent Sammy to look for 'a left-handed screwdriver' on his first day. Sammy had fallen for it.

"Okay," Pavel said, sighing out the word. "No real harm done, Sammy. We can make good, fix it. But next time, son, you make sure you check with me, or one of the other guys, before you drill a hole. In anything. Right?"

“Right, boss,” replied Sammy, staring down at his steel-capped work boots. “Sorry.”

My first proper job, he thought. *And I’m making a right pig’s breakfast of it.*

Pavel slapped him on the shoulder and helped him change the bit on the masonry drill. Then the foreman watched carefully as Sammy drilled the next hole in the sandstone wall. Sammy should have been grateful, he knew that. Pavel had been patient, considerate, and never lost his rag for long. But somehow, he still resented the foreman, almost hated him. Again, thoughts he knew were wrong, unreasonable, kept surfacing as he worked.

Bloody foreigners, coming over here, taking our jobs, giving us orders. Always finding fault. Why don’t they all go back where they came from?

Sammy had heard others express the same views of migrant workers from Europe, and further afield. But he had always been easygoing, someone who made friends with anyone regardless of race, creed, color. Yet, since he had started working at Rookwood, he struggled to be cheerful, upbeat. Dark thoughts seemed to invade his mind, unless he was always on the alert to stop them, turn them aside.

Like something is stopping me being myself.

Sammy pushed the masonry drill forward gently against the heart of another chalked X. He felt the stone resist. He smiled as the powerful tool cut into the surface, defeating it, penetrating it. Sammy felt an odd, uplifting sensation, an awareness of the power he wielded. He applied more pressure, smiled as he overcame the stone, relishing the raw power of the drill.

I’ll show them, he thought. *I’ll show them all what I’m made of.*

***

The girl took a couple of paces into the room, then spoke again.

“Hello,” she said. “I’m Liz.”

Paul walked over to her, extending a hand as he introduced himself. She reached out, and he felt the cool grip of small fingers. She withdrew her hand quickly.

"Pleased to meet you," she murmured, looking up at him, her expression suddenly serious. "You're American. Or from Canada."

"USA," he said, "but I've been here a good while now. Warm beer, fish and chips—I love 'em all."

Liz looked puzzled for a moment, then laughed.

"I've never met an American," she said. "You're quite handsome, I suppose. Are you a millionaire?"

Paul struggled to think of a reply, then Liz laughed again.

"Sorry," she said. "I can be quite silly sometimes. Are you going to live here?"

She half-walked, half-danced across the apartment to the window, gestured out at the view. Paul was startled by how animated the girl seemed all of a sudden. He caught himself checking out the contours of her young body as she moved inside the sack-like dress. She was, he noted, fuller-figured than her slender arms and legs suggested.

Liz looked him squarely in the eye, put a finger to her lips, made a coy face. He felt himself grow red in the face.

Caught me looking, he thought. *Now she's in flirt mode.*

"Um, I guess I might move in," he told her. "I haven't really decided yet."

"I hope you do," she replied. "It would be nice to have someone—someone nice, to talk to. I get lonely sometimes."

Paul was about to ask how someone so young came to be living alone in a high-end apartment but stopped himself. He had learned from many awkward moments that the British did not like such direct questions. And there was something else. For all her playfulness, Liz had an air of melancholy.

"I have to go!" she said abruptly. "But I'll see you again, won't I?"

Before Paul could stammer out an answer she had moved with startling quickness from the window, past him, and out of the door. A moment later he heard the voices of Kate Bewick and Sadie Prescott growing louder. He went outside the flat, looked both ways. The motion-sensitive lights were just switching off to the left. Then, to the right, lights came on as Kate and Sadie rounded the corner, the latter still talking animatedly.

The stairway was opposite the front door of apartment 212. Paul caught a glimpse of a small figure watching him from around the corner and thought for a moment that it might be Liz. Then he realized that it was a much younger girl, a child, in fact, her eyes huge in a heart-shaped face. He began to smile, raise a hand to wave, but the girl was already gone.

"I'll make sure Declan gets onto it," Kate was saying. "But now I must attend to Doctor Mahan."

Sadie Prescott looked at Paul with more interest than before.

"Doctor?" she said. "I've got terrible osteoarthritis in my left knee—"

"My doctorate is in American history," he cut in, smiling apologetically. "Sorry, no medical knowhow."

Sadie looked at him in mild disappointment.

"Oh well," said Sadie, "it was nice meeting you."

Kate and Paul watched the formidable woman set off down the stairs. When she was out of sight, they exchanged knowing smiles.

"Guess she takes up a lot of your time?" Paul asked.

Kate shrugged, and asked him if he needed to know anything else about the apartment. Paul again sensed her borderline desperation to close a deal and wondered how many people had declined signing up to live at Rookwood.

Am I going to turn this place down because of its history, plus a few teething troubles? Paul asked himself. *That would make me a coward and an idiot.*

"No," he said, "I've seen enough. I'll take it. I can move in right away."

Kate looked up at him with apparent disbelief, but that soon gave way to pleasure. She ushered him downstairs to her office where various documents were ready to be signed. As he went through the formalities Paul chatted with Kate, trying to stay focused on sensible, grown-up matters. But in his mind's eye, he kept seeing Liz, her slightly immature face, the way her body filled out her nondescript dress.

For God's sake, he thought. *You're thirty-six, you can't drool over teenagers. Imagine she were one of your students.*

CHAPTER 2

Declan lifted the plastic sheeting that marked the end of the habitable area of Rookwood. From now on he was on a building site. He picked up a hard hat from a small pile on a bench.

"Safety first," he murmured, as he settled the plastic dome onto his hairless scalp. "Ironic if you got killed by a bit of dodgy scaffolding."

Declan had worked construction in Belfast in his youth. He could tell the men currently refurbishing the East Wing were a mix of experience and incompetence. He felt some sympathy for the Polish foreman, Pavel, who had been saddled with a less than brilliant outfit.

Poor bugger has to spend too much time supervising, correcting mistakes, Declan thought. *That always slows work to a snail's pace.*

Declan picked his way past piles of debris and building materials. He could tell from unopened packages and untouched items that work had not progressed very far. The place was stark, dirty, and felt chilly despite the June sunshine outside. Declan paused to look out of one of the unglazed windows. He saw Kate Bewick showing the American guy out to her car.

No doubt she'll give him a lift to the Metro station, he thought, walking on. *She's so desperate to make her quota, she'd probably shag him senseless on her desk.*

Declan stopped, surprised and dismayed. He had never thought harshly of Kate before, but the prurient image had flashed into his mind. He felt ashamed, and an irrational fear that someone knew his sordid thoughts.

It's this place, he thought. *I wish I'd known more about it before I took the job.*

The piercing whine of a drill biting into stone shook him out of his unpleasant reverie. He walked on, saw movement inside a room, waved as a face turned toward him. It was one of the men he did not like much. Doug, a local with an unsubtle sense of humor; had a propensity for what he called Irish jokes. He would trot out some outdated stereotype about what he called 'our Celtic cousins', then add 'No offense!' as if the phrase was some kind of protective charm.

"Hey, there, Doug, how's it going?" he asked, raising his voice above the noisy drilling.

"Not so bad," Doug replied, putting down his tools. "Another day, another dollar, as they say."

Declan looked at the wall that Doug had been plastering. The work was barely adequate, nothing like as good as that in the rest of Rookwood. Rather than comment on the slipshod work, Declan asked if the team had experienced any electrical problems. Doug shrugged.

"Not that I know of," he said. "Why?"

Declan gave an evasive answer and made to go on, wanting to talk to Pavel. But there was a lull in the drilling and Doug, predictably, took advantage of it.

"Hey," he said, "here's a good one. Mrs. Murphy goes up to Father O'Malley, and she's all crying and upset, and she says, 'Oh Father, my husband passed away last night!' So, the priest says, 'Oh Mary, that's terrible! Did he have any last requests?' And she says—"

"For Christ's sake put the gun down," cut in Declan, smiling thinly and heading for the doorway. "See you later, Doug."

"What do you call an Irishman sitting on a couch?" demanded Doug.

"Paddy O'Furniture," Declan shot back. "Get some new material, pal."

Typical bloody Brit, he thought bitterly, as he made his way back out of the East Wing. *Too damn stupid to know how stupid he is.*

***

The main gates had been left open. "There are some pending lawsuits over the electrical systems," Kate remarked. "But of course, everything moves so slowly. In the meantime, any problems, just get in touch with Declan or me."

Paul nodded, distracted by someone standing on the opposite side of the road. It was a white-haired woman of around sixty. She was apparently staring at the gates of the apartment complex. As Kate's car turned onto Blaydon Avenue, Paul found himself looking into the woman's dark eyes. She seemed vaguely familiar, and he wondered if she had some connection to the university. Then they had passed her, and Paul saw her still figure receding in the wing mirror.

"Somebody seems fascinated by Rookwood," he commented.

"Oh?" Kate replied. "I didn't notice."

After she had dropped him off at Temple Grove station Paul had a six-minute wait for the next train into Tynecastle. He wandered restlessly up and down the platform, wondering if he had made the right decision. Finally, he called his friend Mike, explained that he no longer needed to crash with him. Mike, to his credit, did not sound too enthusiastic about Paul moving out and offered to help.

"What's the place like, anyway?" Mike asked. "Any top tottie? This Kate woman sounds a bit of all right?"

"You're a Seventies throwback, Mike," Paul answered, smiling. "After what I went through with Mari, you think I'm just going to dive into another relationship?"

"Relationship?" Mike's voice rose an octave. "Mate, you need to get back on the horse, get your leg over. Nothing complicated, just a good bit of old fashioned—"

"Gotta go, train's here," Paul said, ending the call. "See you later. I'll bring a celebration curry, plus a bottle of something."

As the train rattled its way through the suburbs of Tynecastle, Paul pondered his next move. He could move most of his stuff out of storage, take up residence in a new home. That fresh start would be the ideal time to begin a much postponed project; his new book.

No more excuses, he told himself. *You've got to get something out there. Publish or perish.*

The train stopped and more passengers got on. A young woman sat opposite Paul. He noticed her short skirt and fine legs in sheer hose. He made himself look out of the window, think of something irrelevant. He recalled the missing cat posters on the trees outside Rookwood. Then he tried to visualize the face of the gray-haired woman.

What was it about her that seemed familiar? Paul wondered. *I must have seen her somewhere before. But where?*

***

"Hey, kid," said Doug. "Want to do me a favor?"

Sammy looked up from his phone. He had wolfed down his sandwich and Snickers bar so he could spend more of his lunch break playing Space Fruit Jamboree. He was about to level up, but he could not ignore a senior worker. And everyone was senior to Sammy.

"Yeah, what's up?" he said cautiously.

"You know that Irish bloke, Declan?" Doug asked. "Well, could you go and find him and ask him if he's got a reversible drill?"

Sammy stood up, put his phone away, and looked suspiciously at Doug. The older man had fooled him before. He had never heard of a reversible drill. Seeing Sammy's expression, Doug held up his hands in a show of contrition.

"Oh, now come on, lad!" Doug protested. "This is important. You see, those oversized holes of yours need to be filled in, and for that, you need a reversible drill. But we ain't got one—not standard equipment, you see. Declan's a general handyman, so he might have one lying about. Get it?"

Sammy nodded reluctantly. Just because he had never heard of a piece of specialist equipment did not mean it didn't exist. And if he refused to help Doug, and Doug complained to the foreman, Pavel might simply sack him. The thought of going home to his mother and little sister gave Sammy a sinking feeling in his stomach.

"Okay," he said. "I'll go and ask."

It's a lie, said a little voice in his head. *It's a dirty trick, a lie, another way of making you look stupid.*

Sammy tried to ignore the voice, but then it was joined by another one. As he made his way out of the East Wing and into the main block, his head seemed to be filling with voices. He stopped in the corridor to put his hands over his ears, but it had no effect. Far from it. The voices grew louder. And they were all telling him the same thing. As the corridor lights winked out, he heard all the voices become one. It was a sneering, superior voice, posh and full of itself.

They are going to get rid of you, Sammy, they are going to ruin your life.

"Shut up!" he hissed, and started to run down the corridor, heading for the foyer, wanting to simply be in the sunlight.

***

"Wow!" exclaimed Mike Bryson. "You really can't afford this. You do know that, right?"

"It's cheaper than it looks," Paul said patiently. "As I've told you many times."

"Well, it's your overdraft," declared Mike, stopping his Peugeot outside Rookwood. "Let's get all your tatty possessions inside this pristine dwelling place, so you can start dragging it down to your level."

Paul had to laugh at that. He had been couch-surfing at Mike's place for over a month, and his friend had not once complained. This was despite Paul's tendency to cover every available surface with books, journals, coffee cups, and the remnants of fast-food meals.

"I'll have to be careful not to mess the place up," he admitted, standing by as Mike opened the trunk of the Peugeot. "All sorts of fancy rules on tenant's behavior."

Mike handed Paul a couple of boxes of books.

"Well, the point is you've got a place of your own now—a fine bachelor pad!"

Both elevators were out of order today. Mike rolled his eyes, asked if there was a service elevator they could use. Paul admitted that he had not asked about that obvious point the previous day. There was nobody in the small office Kate used. They put the boxes down and went in search of Declan, who almost ran into them as he emerged from his office.

"Ah, sorry fellas," he said, when Paul explained the problem. "But the service elevator is on the blink as well. I can help you shift anything awkward, furniture and that, just give me a call."

Paul put Declan's number into his phone. As he finished, he looked past the Irishman, then stared. A large group of people seemed to be advancing along the corridor toward them in semi-darkness. It was a menacing sight, and Paul felt a sudden irrational frisson. Then the lights flickered, and all he could see was one moon-faced young man in workman's clothes. Declan turned, greeted the stranger as Sammy.

"See you later," Paul said. "Gotta get working on that slipped disc."

As they began the climb to the second floor Mike began to ask about neighbors. Paul decided not to mention Liz.

Besides, he thought. *I'm not sure if she actually lives here. She didn't say she did, not in so many words.*

"You've gone a bit quiet," said Mike, over his shoulder. "Not having second thoughts, are we?"

"Nah," Paul responded. "I've got a good feeling about this. Fresh start, fresh challenges. It's all good."

Perhaps it was just being in the stairwell, but Paul thought his voice sounded hollow.

***

"Are you sure it's a reversible drill you're wanting, son?" Declan asked. "Not a tin of striped paint, say? Or how about a long stand?

Maybe I could do you a pail of steam, since I'm at a loose end?"

Sammy felt the sinking feeling again, butterflies in his stomach. He had been made a fool of, again. He was away from work, and his lunchbreak was over. Pavel might even now be wondering where he was, cursing the useless apprentice. Declan, seeing Sammy's expression, smiled wanly and touched his arm lightly.

"Ah, it was that Doug that sent you, wasn't it?"

Sammy nodded.

"That bastard," said Declan, "trying to drop you in it. I'll come back with you, have a word with Pavel, how would that be?"

Sammy shook his head, unable to speak, shook off the Irishman's hand. Anger, a volcanic rage that he had never felt before, seemed to possess him and drive all thoughts from his head. His vision seemed to fail for a moment, his surroundings growing darker, blurred, awash with shadows. Shadows that spoke.

They'll never give you a chance, any of them. It's just like at school, making fun of the stupid boy, mocking you, so unfair.

Sammy could only just hear Declan talking to him, see the Irishman's concerned expression. The builder turned away, began to walk back towards the East Wing. Around him the shadows crowded, faces just visible at the edge of his vision, words filling his mind with anger, hatred, despair. He felt himself swept along on a tide of exultant rage, and gradually, all that was Sammy was washed away. What was left was a shell inhabited by dozens of minds that jostled and bickered for control.

Sammy, now a spectator in his own body, watched himself push through the plaster-spattered plastic sheeting. He was in the East Wing proper now, and the voices in his head grew louder, more strident. They called for revolt, for blood, for death and destruction. Part of Sammy still wanted to resist their call, to do the right thing. But the mob infesting his skull was too strong, too loud, too full of rage.

Rage at the living. The dead are so angry.

Sammy saw Doug, smirking, his mouth moving, a finger pointing.

The chorus of fury was too loud to make out anything Doug said, and soon the jokester was frowning, clearly puzzled, asking a question. Sammy walked right past him, into the old operating theater where Pavel and the others were working. Pavel frowned, asked a question, but again, Sammy could not hear him. Instead, he walked over to the masonry drill, picked it up, turned, walked back out of the room.

Doug was coming along the corridor, smirking again, but this time the mocking smile faltered. Sammy felt his arms raise the drill, press a finger down on the button. Even with the furious roar of the voices in his head, the powerful whine of the motor was still audible. It sounded good. It sounded inevitable, as if everything had been leading up to this moment of blood and pain and terror.

Doug reacted too slowly. He was still walking towards Sammy, still bringing himself into danger when he realized what was about to happen. Doug flung up a hand and the drill tore into fingers, sending flesh flying against the walls. Blood spattered over Sammy's face. His body lunged forward, the raging mob not caring if he fell, if his stolen body was injured. The important thing, the only thing, was to drive the whirring metal into Doug.

Sammy, still a spectator, felt a thrill of horror mingled with satisfaction as the drill did its work.

CHAPTER 3

"Hello!" said Mike. "I think one of your neighbors is checking you out."

Paul thought of Liz, and almost dropped the boxes he was carrying. It was not the pale girl, but an actual child Mike was talking about. The girl had ginger hair, huge blue eyes, and was wearing a dark school uniform. Paul realized she was the child who had been peeping at him earlier.

"I'm Mike, what's your name?"

The girl looked up at Mike with a disapproving expression.

"Children are not supposed to talk to strange men," she said. "You know that."

Mike looked abashed, but only for a moment.

"I'm not strange," he protested. "Just a bit peculiar at times. And my transatlantic friend here is as respectable as they come."

Mike indicated Paul, who smiled at the girl. Now that he could see her more clearly, the child he had caught watching him when he had been viewing the apartment before looked a little skinny, undersized, her expression wary. The school uniform seemed slightly shabby, with traces of what might have been oatmeal on the black-and-green plaid skirt. The girl was standing on the landing peering at them, and behind her the door to an apartment was open. A woman's voice called out.

"Ella? Who are you talking to?"

"Just some men," Ella replied. "They're moving boxes. One says he's peculiar."

"Just moving in, upstairs," Mike called. "Nothing strange about us, honest."

The woman who emerged from the flat was plump, with flaming red hair braided into what looked like a copper cable hanging down her dark jacket. Her manner was harassed, her expression slightly hostile.

But Brits often look like that when you first meet 'em, Paul thought.

Mike, always garrulous, introduced them both. The woman still looked sour, but had no option but to reciprocate. She was Neve Cotter, her daughter was Ella, and they were running late. There was a meaningful pause as Neve waited for the men to get out of her way. Then mother and child were gone, with just a perfunctory 'Good Morning' from Neve. Ella gave Paul a long, appraising look just before she turned the corner of the stairwell.

"You could be in there," Mike said. "Overworked single mothers, they can't afford to be picky when it comes to dating."

Paul shook his head in mock despair. Since Paul had split with Mari, Mike had spent almost every waking hour telling his friend to get back into the dating scene. Paul had repeatedly pointed out that he had no intention of doing anything of the kind. Mike ignored him.

"Seriously, mate," Mike said, as he dumped his boxes in the middle of Paul's new living room. "You need to get back on the pony."

"Don't you mean the horse?" Paul asked.

"Baby steps," Mike shot back. "Start small. Get to know the redhead on the first floor, try out a few lines, maybe invite her round for dinner."

"I need to actually move in first," Paul pointed out. "And since there's no working elevator, that might be difficult. What with me needing a bed, and so forth. In the meantime, let's at least get the rest of the stuff out of your car."

The ambulance arrived just as they reached the bottom of the stairs, its piercing siren rendering all talk impossible. Declan was standing in the foyer, hands covered in blood, standing by a flustered-looking Kate Bewick. The siren cut out, paramedics rushed in, and the manager proceeded to lead them towards the East Wing.

"Has there been an accident?" Mike asked.

Declan looked at the Englishman, pale-faced, clearly confused.

"I went after him," he stammered. "I thought the lad was looking upset, a bit out of it, so I went after him. If I'd been a bit quicker—"

Declan looked at his hands.

"We should get you cleaned up," Paul said, speaking gently. "Is there a washroom?"

As Declan washed the blood off, he tried to describe what he had seen. Paul gathered that a building worker had seriously injured, or maybe killed, a colleague. Paul, standing in the doorway of the washroom, peered out as the paramedics carried out a stretcher. The figure on it had its head covered.

"Guess he's dead," Paul said quietly. "Jesus, that's awful."

"Too right," Mike replied, craning to see. "But look who's coming now."

A police car was drawing up. Declan, who had finished drying his hands, froze when he saw it, and Paul noticed the Irishman move sideways, putting Mike between him and the door. Kate Bewick met the two uniformed officers at the door, then ushered them along. Once the cops were out of sight Declan seemed to relax and led the friends back to his office.

"So, was it deliberate?" Mike asked, as Paul poured boiling water into three mugs. The smell of instant coffee filled the small room.

"Looks like it," said the caretaker. "But it's bloody insane. That lad was as meek as a—as a lamb. Not too bright, maybe, but nice enough. And now this."

"You mean he attacked someone?" Paul asked.

Declan nodded.

"It was bloody carnage in there, man!" he whispered. "I've not seen anything like it since—for a long time."

Mike produced a hip flask and poured a measure of 'the good stuff' into Declan's mug. The Irishman thanked him, took a gulp, choked slightly. Again, Paul noticed the patch where the tattoo had been erased but decided not to ask about it. Instead, Paul and Mike between them coaxed out some details of the incident.

"There have been accidents before," Declan added. "It's why the

East Wing's still not finished. Everything goes wrong there. Power surges, floorboards giving way, the roof collapsing. Bloody place is jinxed. If it was up to me, I'd just knock it down, make do with the other two blocks."

Mike slapped Paul on the back.

"Well done, pal," he said with mock-heartiness. "You've moved into a cursed asylum."

"Piss off, Mike," Paul replied sourly. "I'm sure it's just a run of bad luck."

Declan finished off his coffee, put the mug down. He looked out of the window, over the pleasant, sunlit turf that fell away toward the gates. A flock of black birds was rising from the lawn. Paul wondered if they were rooks.

"Maybe it is bad luck, but—this place," Declan hesitated, then went on. "It's got a reputation. East Wing especially, but the whole place—the history is dark, not pleasant. I looked into it at first, then I stopped looking."

Voices in the corridor told them that Kate was on her way back, accompanied by the police. Declan stiffened, and Paul saw a hint of panic in the caretaker's face. Then the Irishman became impassive, took a breath, straightened up.

"All right, gentlemen," Declan said. "Best get along or the Peelers will be taking statements, wasting your bloody time. And yes, you can move the rest of your stuff up. Business as usual, eh?"

In the event, the police showed no interest in questioning anyone and departed a few minutes later. The construction workers left shortly afterward. Declan pitched in to help Paul and Mike finish up faster and told them the workers would not be back.

"They quit?" Paul asked, surprised. "I'd have thought they couldn't afford to just walk off the job."

"The foreman just gave up," Declan explained. "He said he couldn't work in these conditions. Kate naturally assumed he was after more money, but when she offered to bump up their bonuses they still buggered off."

They finished moving boxes to Paul's apartment, and Declan promised to chase up the 'useless wankers' who were supposed to fix the elevators. He predicted that Paul would be able to get his furniture out of storage in 'a week or so, tops'. Paul thanked the caretaker but wondered if he would really be moving in soon. He remarked, half seriously, that the jinx on Rookwood seemed to be hindering him a little.

"Ah, it'll all work out," Mike said cheerfully as they stepped out into the sunlight. "And when you do move out of my place, you will miss my home cooking. I can always bring one of my famous curries round for the housewarming."

"I can feel my stomach rejoicing at the mere thought," grimaced Paul.

He glanced up at the front of the building and saw a face at a window. It was looking down at him from the second floor. He thought it might be Liz, and took a step back, shielding his eyes, but the glare from the sunlight meant he could not make out any features. Then the face was gone.

"Come on," Mike said, "we passed a promising pub about a mile down the road. See if they do real ale, decent grub."

As they drove out of the gates Paul saw a familiar figure standing on the curb opposite. It was the gray-haired woman, her eyes concealed by sunglasses, but still apparently staring at Rookwood.

"Former inmate, you reckon?" asked Mike.

The offhand question surprised Paul. He had never thought that any of the asylum's patients might still be alive. But, he reasoned, if it closed down in the Fifties it was possible that people who had been committed to Rookwood might still be around.

"I guess it's possible," he conceded, looking back at the motionless woman. "Or, of course, she could be a former staff member. Maybe worked as a nurse, cleaner, cook or whatever."

Mike soon lost interest in the topic, and in a couple of minutes, they had arrived at the pub.

***

The short interview with the police left Declan nervous, wondering how deeply they would dig into his background. He knew the police were short-handed and snowed under with paperwork. Declan was almost sure he had not given them any grounds for suspicion. But then, there were witnesses to what had happened. It all seemed clear enough.

And it's not the cops you need to worry about, put in the unwelcome, insinuating voice in his head. *Not really. Is it?*

"Shut up," he muttered, wishing the American's pal had left his hip flask. "Just shut up."

Declan always tried to find something to do, however trivial, when bad memories threatened to well up. He called the maintenance company again, got a terse reply. He called on Sadie Prescott to fix a dripping tap. As usual, Sadie flirted with him in a half-serious way, but Declan wasn't in the mood for the game.

Stop putting it off, said the small voice. *You have to go eventually. It's your job, Declan.*

"Bugger off!" he said, leaning back in his office chair, adding to his digital log.

"Erm, I beg your pardon?" said Kate Bewick.

Declan jumped up, wondering how the woman managed to move so quietly.

"Sorry!" he said hastily. "Swearing at the computer, and the modern world in general."

"You're forty-five, Dec," Kate said flatly, showing no inclination to banter. "I think we should check out—check out what the situation is."

Declan knew what she meant but did not want to admit it. He suddenly felt like a frightened little boy again. He shook off his fear, or at least wrestled it down long enough to stand up and follow Kate. As they walked toward the entrance to the East Wing, she talked about all her problems. Mostly, she bemoaned her inability to get workers to stay on the job, the pressure from the company head office in London, and the general cussedness of events.

"These big blokes with their toolbelts, all very macho, but you'd think they were six-year-olds, some of them," she complained. "Seeing things, hearing things, getting the shivers. At least you're sensible, Dec."

"Don't go calling me sensible now," he said, trying to sound insouciant. "That'll ruin a reputation it's taken me years to—"

He fell silent as he saw a smeared, almost black handprint on the wall ahead. It was almost certainly his, made with the dried blood of the victim. Declan tried not to think of the great fan of bright red blood that had sprayed from the workman's chest. Declan had grabbed Sammy, tried to pull the drill away. Others had helped, but somehow Declan had ended up with bloody hands. He could not quite recall how.

The Red Hand, said the little, sneering voice. *Now, that's the symbol of the brave province of Ulster, is it not?*

"Pure coincidence," he muttered.

Kate paused in the doorway, frowning at him.

"Come on, Dec," she said, impatient now. "I need you to check on what's been left undone, what needs to be fixed straight away. I've got to file a report."

"Right, sure, okay."

The manager hesitated, feeling guilty, then put a hand on his arm.

"I'm sorry, Dec," Kate said. "You can take a couple of days to get over it, no problem. Just help me out now, please."

Declan followed Kate through the bloodstained plastic curtain. As soon as he set foot on the old, cracked tiles of the East Wing, he felt a distinct chill. It was like standing near an open fridge door. He fastened a shirt button, almost turned up his collar, as Kate started to point at various incomplete jobs and ask questions. Declan did his best to assess any safety issues but kept being distracted. The spatter patterns of blood on the walls were almost hypnotic, constantly luring his attention away from more practical matters.

"Okay," Kate sighed, "let's move on. I guess we're both a bit squeamish about—about all this."

Declan felt himself relax slightly. At least the other rooms and corridors would be blood-free. He followed the manager out of the bloody chamber, wondering if a regular cleaning firm would be willing to tackle it. He stopped to glance back and assess just how much gore required removal.

Holy Mother of God.

"Declan? What is it now? I've got a teleconference at three, we need to get this done. What are you staring at?"

He felt Kate walk up to stand just behind him. She fell silent as soon as she saw what he had seen. Across the wall above the doorway that led into the East Wing were letters, apparently daubed in blood onto fresh plaster. The message was both clear and baffling, a straightforward English phrase that made no sense to Declan at all.

TELL ANNIE'S STORY

***

That evening, Neve Cotter told some necessary half-truths to her daughter. A man had had a bad accident, she explained, and the other workmen had decided they did not want to stay. This was Neve's edited version of the gossipy account spread by Sadie Prescott via text and email. She hoped other children at school would not give more information, that Ella would not be shown anything too disturbing on the internet.

Ella, a quiet child, looked appraisingly at her mother and asked a series of questions. No, Neve did not know when the workmen would come back. Yes, sometimes people did die after accidents. No, she did not know why God permitted bad things to happen. Perhaps Ella could ask Father Carswell in Sunday School.

Ella looked skeptical. Neve wondered for a moment if she had played the priest card once too often.

"Anyhow, young lady, tell me about school today. And not in monosyllables!"

As Ella gave a precise account of her day, Neve checked the mail she had picked up on her way in. There was the usual array of bills, junk mail, and a couple of letters. One was from Neve's mother and contained a twenty-pound banknote 'to buy a little something for Ella'. Neve sighed, knowing she would have to call her mother or be called within forty-eight hours. The last piece of mail had a printed address label, a second-class stamp that was slightly askew. As she opened it, Neve held her breath.

It can't be, she told herself. *It can't be from him.*

The letter was printed, but signed in a familiar, immature scrawl. It was from her ex-boyfriend, Jeff.

> *I hope you and Ella have settled in okay. I think it's a pity that you walked out on me without leaving me a forwarding address. Sets a bad example for the kid, and it hurt my feelings. Are you trying to turn Ella against me? Me and you had something good, babe, and now you're pretending it never happened? I don't like that. No man would, and I'm a man, not a doormat, as you well know. Take care.*

Neve crumpled the letter, made to put it into a wastepaper basket. Then she thought of Ella finding it and becoming scared again. She shoved it into the pocket of her jeans. Ella stopped listing things she had done and asked what was for dinner. Neve looked at her daughter for a long moment.

"Whatever you want today," she said.

"Can we order pizza?" asked Ella immediately. "And are you being nicer because Jeff found us again?"

***

Three days later, Declan contacted Paul to tell him the service elevator was fixed. Paul arranged to have his furniture moved from storage into the apartment. Media coverage of the 'accident' at Rookwood had faded away, but Paul still felt some nagging doubt at the official statement. An inexperienced teenager was said to have accidentally killed another man. A coroner's inquest would be convened in due course. Meanwhile, according to Kate Bewick, work on the East Wing was suspended until another contractor could be found.

"I get the feeling," Paul said, scrolling through the latest updates, "that a lot of people want this to just go away. Apart from the family of the poor bastard who died, of course."

"Nothing for you to worry about," said Mike, looking over Paul's shoulder. "It's not like you're going to be operating a pneumatic drill or something."

Paul closed the news app, laid his phone down on the kitchen table. There was barely room for it amid plates, cups, and pages from the morning newspaper. The clutter all around was a permanent reminder that Mike had allowed his friend to stay over for weeks in a one-person flat. Rent free.

"It's their management I'm worried about," Paul explained. "They seem to have a lot of accidents, failures, breakdowns—I can do without that sort of hassle."

Mike did not look up from the football pages.

"But look on the bright side, that Kate's a bit of all right," he opined. "So, if you've got plenty of excuses to go and talk to her, maybe Cupid will find a target for one of his little arrows."

Paul laughed uncomfortably. Rookwood's manager was attractive, he agreed. But the thought of initiating any kind of relationship with a confident, career-woman type was daunting. Kate was far too similar to

Mari, in fact.

"Do you never think of anything else?" he asked, by way of deflection.

Mike held up the newspaper.

"I worry about Liverpool's fortunes in the Premiership," he said. "That, along with work and sex, pretty much fill up my waking hours."

Paul got up, tipped the remains of his breakfast into the trash, and ran the plate under a hot tap.

"You are such a slob," Mike commented. "Stand aside, newly-single guy, and let me do the washing up. One of the many civilized skills you will need to cultivate when you're finally living on your own."

It was a throwaway remark. But for the rest of the day, Paul found himself dwelling on the simple thought. In the middle of a tutorial on the Monroe Doctrine, he lost the thread of a student's argument. He was visualizing Apartment 212 at Rookwood; empty, cold, unwelcoming.

Living alone. Walking into a home where nobody else lives.

He realized the young people around the table were staring at him.

"Sorry, people," he said. "Let's try that one again."

***

Jeff Bowman had walked up from the Metro station, hoping to spy out the terrain, perhaps catch a glimpse of Neve, Ella, or both. He had not expected the gates to Rookwood to be open. On the Rookwood website, the apartment building had been presented as a 'secure place to live' with 'state of the art security measures'. But so far as Jeff could see it was as about as secure as a public library.

Good, he thought. *This will make it a lot easier.*

A large van with the logo of a local moving firm appeared and turned into the gates. It occurred to Jeff that this would cause the usual disturbance and confusion at the entrance. He might, if he was careful, be able to sneak in. However, he did not know how tight security might be at the entrance.

Should I risk it? If it goes wrong and the cops get involved—

Jeff stopped, startled. He had nearly walked straight into a woman who was standing on the edge of the pavement. He felt a moment of irritation, but then noticed that the woman was paying him no heed. Instead, she was peering at Rookwood. Jeff estimated her age to be around sixty-five or seventy, and wondered if she was suffering from dementia.

If I help her, maybe take her home, it proves I'm a good citizen, he thought. A good bloke, not some kind of scumbag.

"Excuse me, but are you all right?" he asked.

The woman gazed up at him. Her eyes were strikingly dark in her pale face, with its halo of silvery-white hair.

"I'm quite all right, young man," the woman replied, tersely. "I was just—"

The woman paused and seemed to reassess Jeff, looking him up and down. He felt slightly self-conscious about his work clothes, faded overalls and scuffed boots. That was followed by a twinge of resentment at the woman for making him feel awkward.

Why do women always have to belittle us?

"Sorry!" he said, raising his hands in placatory gesture. "Just thought you looked a bit—worried."

The woman snorted, and Jeff thought she was going to say something to demean him.

"We should all be worried about that place," she said. "It's troubled. Everybody knows that. If you're thinking of taking a job there, don't."

She stomped off along the street, heading downhill towards the Metro. Jeff watched her go, lost for words. He wondered if she was slightly crazy. Jeff had heard some vague stories about Rookwood but was far too preoccupied with the injustices he had suffered. But the woman had also planted the seed of an idea.

Taking a job there, he thought. *I'm a qualified electrician, why couldn't I just bluff my way in?*

Jeff smiled to himself as he watched the moving men start to unload items from their van. It was as if a solution to his problem had been handed to him by some higher power. He had a plan. As he set off back into Tynecastle he began to work out some of the details. It was not flawless, but it could work.

Then we'll see who's in the right, he thought, as he turned to walk back to the station. *Then we'll see who's in the wrong. That lying bitch will regret smearing me, blackening my name. Turning the child against me.*

CHAPTER 4

Paul moved in on Friday afternoon.

Mike helped bring in the last of Paul's possessions, and then went out to get a celebratory pizza, plus some beer. The two spent a few hours 'shooting the breeze', as Mike insisted on calling it.

"It's not a term I ever use," Paul pointed out, not for the first time. "Like I never say 'hubba hubba'. Nor have I been heard to utter the phrase, 'Aw, shucks.' In fact, I am more likely to say, 'Pip pip, old bean, have a buttered scone.'"

"Hot diggety," Mike shot back. "Somebody is awfully sensitive."

Paul frowned at his empty beer bottle, got up, and walked unsteadily into the kitchen. As he opened the fridge he shouted back at Mike.

"Mocking my American ethnicity is against university policy," he declared. "In fact, the next time you exclaim 'Dagnabbit!', I will file a formal complaint."

Mike made a disrespectful noise.

"Bring two bottles," he added.

"Only one left," Paul said. "God, I have not been so drunk in—well, maybe I've never been so drunk."

We're coming to the end of our little party, he thought. *My first guest in my new home will be going soon.*

Paul realized, with a flush of shame, that he did not want Mike to leave. The thought of being left alone amid empty bottles and fragments of pizza almost sobered him up. He stumbled through an attempt to thank Mike for all his help. This, predictably, sped up the Englishman's departure.

"Don't go all sentimental on me," insisted Mike. "You'll help me out one day, I bet."

Paul closed the door and walked unsteadily back into his new living room. He knew what was coming next. Despite the beer, or perhaps because of it, depression would come. He had fought against it for many years, but the breakup with Mari had brought a wave of bleak thoughts and feelings. It did not take much to bring a sense of hopelessness bubbling up, almost swamping his mind.

I can beat it, he told himself. *I've beaten it before.*

He switched on the TV, channel surfed, and found a dumb action movie. He made himself a coffee while heroes and villains fought a deafening gun battle, with a few immense explosions thrown in. The moronic adventure failed to engage him, though. Paul felt emotionally dead.

God, this is worse than before, he thought. *Maybe I should go out, take a walk, get some air. Might meet that Declan guy, or Kate, and have a chat.*

He turned the TV off, gulped down the last of his coffee, and got up. At the same moment, he heard a faint knocking noise. Paul stood listening for a moment, but the sound was not repeated. He went to his door and, still unsteady thanks to the beer, looked through the peephole. He could see nobody standing outside in the dim-lit hallway.

Shrugging, he grabbed his keys and opened the door, aiming to head down the stairs, but almost collided with a diminutive figure. For a second, Paul got the impression of a child in a loose, ill-fitting kind of robe. There was also a distinctive odor, not too pleasant, that vanished even as he wrinkled his nostrils in distaste.

Paul's movement seemed to trigger the hallway lights. The shadows were banished, and he recognized Liz, still in her gray dress and nondescript, flat shoes. The girl was looking up at him, smiling hesitantly.

"Oh, hi!" he said, stepping back, out of her personal space. "I didn't see you through the spy-hole thingy."

"I just came to welcome you," she said. "I'm glad you've come here to live."

"Thanks!" he replied. "Um, would you like to come in for a coffee or tea?"

She did not reply but stepped inside. Liz looked around, exclaiming at the number of books he had, looking curiously at his desk with its laptop and charging cell phone. Then she stopped in front of the TV, head tilted to one side.

"Not a big screen," he said ruefully. "Kind of obsolete, I guess."

Liz looked at him strangely.

"We never had a television. A lot of the neighbors got them when the Queen—I mean, a lot of people had them. But my mother said they were ungodly. An offense against decency."

"Wow," he said, struggling to think of an intelligent reply. "But you don't live with your mom now?"

Liz shook her head.

"No, I'm on my own now. Well, sort of."

There was an awkward silence until Paul suggested she sit down. Liz kicked off her shoes and curled up on the sofa. He found it hard to ignore her slender, shapely legs, so made a point of looking past her left ear as he asked her again if she wanted anything.

"A cup of tea would be nice," she said softly. "And a chocolate biscuit, if you have any."

"Cookies? Guess I have some," he said. "Somewhere. Maybe."

He walked over to the kitchen door, stumbled slightly, cursed under his breath.

"You're a little bit drunk, Paul."

"More than a little, I'm afraid!"

He smiled back at Liz, but she was looking at him with a serious expression he could not read. He put a teabag in a mug, poured boiling water over it, and let it brew while he looked for cookies. Eventually, he found a half-empty packet of chocolate digestives, a British 'biscuit' that he sometimes dunked in his coffee.

"Are you lonely?"

Paul dropped the packet, fragments of brittle, light brown biscuit spraying over the tiled floor. Liz was right behind him. Her face showed concern and some puzzlement. She ignored his efforts to pick up the debris. He noticed she was barefoot, and in his half-drunk state he stared at her small, perfectly formed feet.

God, he thought, *inviting her in was a bad idea. I'm gonna make a fool of myself.*

"I asked, are you lonely?"

Paul gave up trying to round up the crumbs on the kitchen floor and stood up again. Looking down at Liz, eyes bleary, he nodded.

"Yeah," he blurted out. "I don't know why exactly, but lately I feel—so alone. I've got a lot to be grateful for, and it's not like it's the first time I've broken up with someone, but—"

Once he had begun talking, all his self-doubt and misery came tumbling out. He felt a cool hand take hold of his, and Liz led him back into the living room. Again, he stumbled, and knew he had had at least one too many with Mike.

"I'm quite drunk," he said, breaking off his account of his struggle with depression. "I'm very drunk, and I'm talking too much. I'm sorry, really, you'd better go."

Liz put a small hand on his forehead. Her skin felt cool, very soft, and Paul thought of a summer breeze caressing him. He closed his eyes, shutting out the evening sunlight that was suddenly too bright.

"Go?" she said. "I want to be here. I want to be with you. We have so much in common."

"Bad idea," he muttered. "Not a good idea to have rebound—to try and—God, I can't even talk now."

"Then don't."

He felt a finger on his lips, then sensed it moving down his chin, his chest. Then she began to unbutton his shirt. Paul mumbled a protest, reached up, and tried to stop the small, agile fingers. But somehow, they seemed far too strong for him.

Oh God, I am so drunk, he thought.

And then he passed out.

***

In his dream, Paul was walking along the hallway outside Apartment 212, heading toward the elevators. The lift doors both bore OUT OF ORDER signs. Paul knew he had to get away, go down to the main entrance, leave Rookwood. He looked up at the stained-glass window, and with dream-logic, implored Saint Dymphna to help him.

The white-robed woman turned her perfect face to his. Her expression held infinite sadness, pity, an understanding of suffering from the inside. The saint, he suddenly realized, was also his mother. He seemed to float, pass through the window, and found himself in a familiar room, a room he hated. It was white-walled, with a pale green carpet, a window looking out onto a snow-bound copse of trees. There was a table, riveted to the floor, and two chairs, also fixed down. Paul sat in one, his mother sat opposite.

His mother was rocking back and forth, slowly, as she always did. She wore a white robe, but it was stained, frayed, nothing like the raiment of a saint in a stained glass. Her hair was disheveled, brownish strands flecked with gray falling over her face. Her eyes peered anxiously at something Paul could not see. He looked down, saw familiar sneakers, a pair he had worn for a couple of summers back in high school. His mother had been in and out of institutions during that time, her body awash with prescription meds, her mind wandering. He had hated visiting her, hated himself for not wanting to go, felt anger and despair at the whole grown-up world for what had happened to her.

Depression.

The word had been woven into the fabric of his life. When they had studied The Great Depression in history class, he had tried hard not to think of his mother staring at the TV, slumped in her robe, not moving or speaking for hours or days. Paul's sisters, older and tougher than he, had held things together for as long as they could. But eventually, Mom had had to 'go away'. They never named the place, never said 'committed'. It was always 'gone away to be looked after properly'.

"Mom?" Paul said. "Mom, it's me."

She looked up because it was a dream. In reality, she had never looked at him, not really. Her face had been turned toward him, but she was seeing some terrible inner world, a private hell he had not understood, not at the time. But now her eyes were focused on him, and she smiled. It was a puzzled, hesitant smile, but Paul still felt immense relief. She had recognized him, she knew him. Then her expression changed to concern, anxiety. Her eyes flickered toward the door. Paul noticed that the door was not as he remembered it. It was metal-framed and padded, covered in worn, studded leather.

"Get out," she said. "Get out, quick."

"Mom?" Paul said.

He felt hurt, rejected. This was as bad as her indifference. He reached out for her hand, but she snatched it away, held it up to the side of her head. And now he saw something new, a patch of redness on her temple, near her left eye. She almost touched it, then let her hand fall.

"Get out before he does this to you," his mother warned. "Get out before the doctor—"

She stopped, her head jerked around, listening. Paul heard the clang of a door opening. A metallic sound like in a prison movie. Then came footsteps, echoing in the corridor outside.

"It's too late," his mother said, shaking her head in despair. "Oh, it's too late. The doctor knows you're here. He knows you're like me. Ready for treatment. Ready for the experiment."

The door opened outward. A flickering, like distant flashes of lightning, played across the wall of the corridor. Then a squat, white-coated figure appeared. Round spectacles reflected the light and made the man's eyes invisible. A surgical mask covered the lower half of his face. The mask rippled as the mouth beneath it spoke.

"It's time for your treatment, Paul. Just like your mother."

The doctor stepped into the room, which was now a padded cell, its floor and walls worn and stained. The chairs and table were gone. So had Paul's mother. Now, he was chained to the wall, and as the masked doctor came closer, he began to pull frantically at his manacles. The doctor held up a hypodermic syringe, tapped it, then tried the plunger. A thin jet of clear fluid shot from the tip of the needle.

"You won't take me back to that place!"

Paul sat up. It took him a moment to realize that he was in his new bedroom. The curtains were open, and a colorless moonlight shone in. He got up, felt his head throb with an incipient hangover. Groaning, he headed to the window, noting that he was still wearing his socks and undershorts. He could make out the distant lights of the city. By his phone, it was just before three in the morning.

What the hell happened?

He flicked on the light and saw his pants and shirt, folded neatly on the chair by the dresser. He recalled Liz, snatches of conversation, the darkness of her eyes, her full-lipped mouth. He remembered her fingers undoing his shirt. He went into the bathroom, winced at the sudden piercing light, and splashed water on his face.

"Okay, you passed out, and a teenage girl put you to bed," he croaked at his reflection. "Possibly a new low."

***

"Why do we have to go to church?" asked Ella.

"Because it's Sunday, and we're Catholics," replied Neve. "Not particularly good ones, but that's all right, because guilt and sin are key parts of the package."

Ella looked up at her mother skeptically.

"But what if I don't believe in God anymore?" she demanded. "Then church is just a man talking."

"Father McGuire will be hurt if you don't go," said Neve, deciding on a change of tactics. "Also, you'll miss all your friends at Sunday School."

Ella looked doubtful, but Neve sensed she was making headway. She continued to fuss around Ella, adjusting her daughter's hair, dress, coat, fretting over the girl's worn school shoes. Then Neve checked her own appearance, groaned at her hair's refusal to remain even vaguely tidy. She decided to shove it all under a woolen hat and hope for the best, then put on her coat.

"I mean, what if after you die there's no heaven or hell?" Ella asked. "What if instead you're just stuck in this world? Doing whatever you were doing before you died?"

Neve paused, frowning at Ella. She had never heard her daughter talk about life and death in this way, let alone the afterlife. She wondered if Ella was coming under the influence of pretentious or morbid friends at school.

"Good people go to heaven," Neve insisted. "We believe that, and it makes sense. Kind of. Now, no more theology because we've got to go!"

They left their flat and headed for the stairs. The American from the second floor was coming down at the same time, dressed in jogging gear. Neve thought he looked terrible, wrung-out, and assumed that he and his English pal had been boozing the night before.

Just what we need, she thought. *Another drunken bloke nearby. And I can't recall his name.*

"Good morning," she said, politely but without warmth.

"Oh, hi!" the American replied, stopping to let Neve and Ella go first. "You heading out for a walk? It's a fine day."

"We're going to church," Neve replied shortly.

"Do you go to church?" Ella asked, looking up at the man.

"Not for a long time," he admitted. "You're Ella, right?"

The girl nodded. Neve resisted the temptation to pull on her daughter's hand, hurry her down the last flight of steps.

"I'm Paul," the American went on. "Guess we're neighbors."

Ella did not reply to that, and Neve felt no desire to talk to Paul. She was sure she could smell beer on his breath, along with sweat. They reached the foyer in awkward silence, and Neve felt relief that the caretaker was there. He seemed to be adjusting an Out of Order sign on one of the elevators.

"Bloody thing's just conked out again," Declan explained, then looked down at Ella. "I reckon somebody messes with them. It wouldn't be you, now, would it miss?"

Ella giggled, and Neve shot her a look.

"Any idea when it'll be fixed?" the American asked.

Declan looked slightly irritated.

"No idea, pal," he said. "But Kate's on the case, I'm sure. And we've still got one working."

Another awkward pause ended when Paul mumbled that he'd better get going. As the American left the building, Declan began chatting with Ella. Neve did not mind. Declan struck her as honest and rather vulnerable in a way. He did not give off a worrying vibe.

Unlike that American, she thought. *There's something about him, something not right.*

"Do you think we go to heaven when we die?" Ella was asking.

Declan looked slightly taken aback, but then grinned.

"Well, of course, we do," he declared. "Except for bad people, like Hitler and Stalin. The Devil, he puts all them fellas on a toasting fork for all eternity."

Ella laughed, and Neve smiled at Declan in gratitude. He always deflected Ella's more serious questions, a skill Neve envied. She gave a gentle tug on Ella's hand, now sure that they were going to be late for morning mass.

"But what about ghosts?" Ella demanded. "How can there be ghosts if people go to heaven?"

Declan's smile seemed to freeze for a moment, then he laughed. It sounded a little forced to Neve.

"Is it ghosts you're frightened of now?" he asked. "I thought a big girl like you would be too sensible for that sort of thing."

"She is," Neve said, forcing a smile of her own. "And we really must run, the service will be starting."

Declan stood and watched as they walked out into the sunlight. Neve suddenly remembered that she had intended to ask him if he would come with them one Sunday. He had described himself as a lapsed Catholic, but Neve felt sure that Declan would benefit from some spiritual help.

He seems so lost and lonely, she thought. *That's sad.*

***

After his encounter with the single mum and her daughter, Paul resolved to lay off the booze for a while. His initial resolve to jog down to the gates of Rookwood and then around the neighborhood soon evaporated, as he felt himself growing short of breath. His fitness regime had gone to hell months ago, when problems with Mari turned to an obvious split in their relationship.

Starting with a five-kilometer run, he thought. *Probably not a brilliant idea. Let's make it about five hundred yards.*

Paul set off to jog slowly around Rookwood, reasoning that he had not looked closely at the place and had only seen it from the front. He went clockwise, circling the West Wing, glancing up occasionally to see if any residents were at their windows. He caught sight of Sadie Prescott watering a window box, called up a cheerful 'Good Morning'. She nodded rather coldly.

I'm earning a ton of disapproval this morning, he thought. *Maybe Mike and me were a little too loud last night?*

The side and back of the West Wing proved uninteresting. However, a small area of woodland came into view, and as Paul gazed at it, a flock of black birds rose with a tremendous cawing and fluttering. Paul assumed they were rooks, and that the wood had given the building its name. He made a note to ask Declan or Kate.

Now he was behind the main block. He looked up to see if he could identify his own apartment. The window looked out over Tynecastle. He slowed to a walk, tried to remember the precise angle.

Corner apartment, second floor, he mused. *So that must be it.*

Someone was looking down at him. Looking at him from his own apartment. He stopped dead, gasped, raised a hand against the bright June sky. The window of the corner flat seemed empty. He dismissed the supposed face as the reflection of a cloud, or something similar.

Jogging on, he made his way past the rear of the main block. Ahead of him he saw movement, what might have been a white-clad figure retreating around the corner. He slowed a little, then sped up again. It might be a child playing a game, or he could simply be mistaken. Sure enough, as he turned the corner, he saw a loose tarpaulin, light gray, moving slightly in the summer breeze.

He slowed to a walk again, examining the East Wing. It showed signs of aborted work. There were windows and doors blocked by plastic sheeting. Piles of bricks and heaps of timber had been abandoned. Paul stopped by a door where the sheeting had been torn back and looked inside.

Shouldn't be doing this, he thought. *May be an unsafe structure.*

Paul took a couple of steps inside the room and shuddered. Despite the balmy summer day, the interior seemed chilly, as if a fridge door had been opened nearby. And yet, the breeze remained gentle, barely moving the stained and smudged plastic sheeting. Paul wondered if anything remained of the old asylum. He felt a sudden, morbid curiosity to see if this old, British institution had resembled the one where his mother had spent so many years.

The plastic covering the doorway opposite bulged out, the sheet flapping. Dust and fragments of plaster were lifted. They floated toward Paul, but he felt no breeze. The sheet rose further, as if someone were pushing it aside. He took a step back, tripped on the uneven floor, reeled into the wall. There was someone else in the room, a figure walking toward him. It was short, thickset, its face half-hidden by an old-style surgical mask. Round glasses gleamed in the half-light. The figure raised a hand, pointed.

The doctor from my nightmare.

"You're not real!" he shouted, closing his eyes.

When Paul looked again, he was alone in the room. He struggled to get upright, brushed plaster dust off his clothes. His hands were shaking, and he laughed nervously at how easily he had been spooked.

Just shadows, he thought. *An optical illusion.*

But something bothered him. If the phantom 'doctor' had been conjured up by his tired, troubled imagination, what had it been pointing at? The figure's plump finger had not been aimed at Paul, but up and to his right. He looked up and saw what seemed to be graffiti, erratic dark brown lettering disfiguring the white wall. Paul craned his neck to make out the words.

"Who the hell is Annie?" he murmured.

CHAPTER 5

Paul sat back and read the paragraphs that had taken nearly an hour for him to write. They were, by any reasonable standard, pretty bad.

> *The British Industrial Revolution created, for many, a new form of serfdom. Where once great feudal lords had brutally dominated the lower classes, now factory owners imposed cruel, inhuman regulations and working conditions on employees. What made the industrial age worse than the predominantly agrarian culture that had preceded it, was the mechanization of many aspects of life. While even the poorest farm laborer could still live according to the natural rhythms of night and day, and the longer cycle of the seasons, factory hands were expected to function as mere extensions of the machines they served. In a supposedly free society, millions of men and women were enslaved by the time clock.*

"Okay, weak and cliched," Paul muttered, "but at least it's coherent."

The next paragraph was altogether stranger. He peered at it, wondering why he could not free himself from grim imaginings.

> *In the grim tenements of London's East End, in the foul hovels of Liverpool and Manchester, disease flourished among malnourished and exhausted families. Violence, incest, and every perversion were*

commonplace, according to social reformers. Madness, too, was prevalent. Rarely a week went by without some godforsaken London slum being visited by commissioners from Bedlam, the notorious asylum. Those unfortunates who were dragged to this hellhole were put on public display, their tormented antics providing a sick form of entertainment for visiting ladies and gentlemen. The physically deformed were also treated as mere exhibits. The most notorious example among many being that of the so-called 'Elephant Man'. The sideshow freak was a staple draw of the traveling circus...

Paul deleted most of the second paragraph. He had begun intending to write a sober academic paper. His topic was the overall effects of industrialization on the health of the Victorian poor. He had a few ideas that, with luck, might draw some attention and get him a little kudos. But no matter how he tried to focus on hard facts, statistics, and learned theories, he kept veering off the point. His mind was haunted by images of suffering and misery, unjust persecution, and mental torment.

"For Christ's sake," he grated, slamming his laptop shut. "You're not writing a goddam Gothic novel!"

He got up and went into the kitchen, got himself a bottle of beer out of the fridge. He had been in this apartment for over a week now and had tried to convince himself that his new home was warm, welcoming, somewhere he could work in peace. But instead, everything seemed to conspire against him achieving anything. When his evenings were not dominated by admin and grading assignments, he found himself unable to write.

"Publish or perish," he said to the empty living room, then took a gulp of beer.

Paul had not published any original research for over a year. He did not have tenure. If he wanted to hold onto his teaching job at Tynecastle U, he had to raise his profile. That meant getting his name into the Journal of Historical Studies, The Nineteenth Century Review, or any of a dozen other prestigious journals. He had come to Rookwood with a ton of good ideas, all neatly filed and annotated. But every time he tried to turn one into a paper, he struggled to stay focused.

"Screw it," he grunted, and slumped onto the sofa. "Looks a lot like perish from where I'm sitting."

There was a brief struggle to find the remote, then he tried to find something to watch that would get his mind off his worries.

***

Ella Cotter had used up her daily quota of iPad time and was now bored. She had done all the reading necessary for school, finished her homework, washed up the dishes, and finished her other chores. She went into the big bedroom, which doubled as Neve Cotter's study, and stood fidgeting until her mother noticed her presence.

"It'll be more fun when you've made some new friends," her mother said, not looking up from her computer. "Now, why don't you watch one of your DVDs?"

Ella did not reply that all her DVDs were for little kids; silly stories about princesses, talking animals, and magic. She had outgrown them. Outgrown was a word she used a lot these days. But Ella knew better than to ask if she could watch TV on her own, because her mother would not risk her seeing something 'upsetting'. Since they had run away from Jeff, Ella's mother had become much more protective.

But I'm not stupid, Ella thought, as she left her mother's bedroom. *I know how to take care and look after myself.*

Ella stopped in the doorway, looking at the evening sunlight slanting across the living room. She decided to test the boundaries, see just how far her mother would let her go.

"Mummy," she said, trying not to sound too enthusiastic, "can I go outside?"

Neve Cotter turned from her screen, gave her daughter an appraising look.

"For some fresh air," Ella went on. "I can go for a nice walk."

For a long moment, the girl was afraid her mother would say no. But then the woman nodded slowly.

"Just so long as you don't go outside the grounds," Neve Cotter warned. "And don't go into the East Wing. And don't pester Declan, or Kate. And don't try to climb any trees—"

The litany of forbidden things went on as Ella put on her shoes and scampered to the front door.

"And be back before eight o'clock!" shouted her mother.

"I will," Ella replied, checking her watch. It was only half past six.

I'll explore the woods, she thought. *I promised I wouldn't climb trees, but I didn't say I wouldn't explore the woods.*

Since they had moved to the edge of the city, Ella had become fascinated by what her mother called creepy-crawlies. She could spend hours watching the behavior of ants, beetles, even worms. Ella wanted to bring some back home in jars or Tupperware but, so far, her mother had been obdurate in refusing.

I'll get her to change her mind, Ella thought, as she closed the front door behind her. *I'll say it's a science project.*

"Hello."

Ella jumped, startled by the voice. The speaker was a girl, but one a lot older than herself. She looked dubiously at the stranger, who was obviously a teenager. Ella knew that most teenagers thought younger kids were boring and didn't want to spend time with them. But this one looked different. It was not just her friendly smile, Ella thought, but the fact that she was dressed like a sensible adult.

The girl wore a knee-length gray dress, flat-heeled black shoes, and her face showed no trace of make-up. That was a surprise for Ella. Most teenage girls in Tynecastle wore what Ella's mother derisively called 'slap'. It made her age hard to guess. Her hair was unusual, too, cut simply in what Ella's grandmother called a bob.

"Hello," Ella replied dubiously, hesitating at the top of the stairs. "I'm just going out to play."

"That's nice," said the girl, sounding a little sad. "I wish I could."

Ella frowned. It was an odd thing for someone to say, especially when they were almost grown up. She wondered if the girl had been grounded by an angry parent. She knew from TV this happened to teenagers a lot.

"You could come out with me," Ella offered. "I go to the woods and—and study natural history.

The strange girl looked puzzled at that.

"You know," Ella went on. "Wildlife. Like Sir David Attenborough."

"Who's he?" the teenager asked. "Does he live around here?"

Ella laughed, then felt slightly ashamed. She wondered if the girl's family were so poor that they couldn't afford TV, computers, any of the things her mother said Ella should be grateful for.

"No," Ella said carefully, "he's on the telly. But I've really got to go."

"I'm Liz," said the girl suddenly, stepping forward, and holding out a pale hand.

Ella looked dubiously at the hand, then smiled, and took it. Her mother had told her to always be polite to adults, and she supposed Liz was at least a borderline case. Liz's hand seemed cold, which was odd on a summer's day. And there was something else, a little tingle of static electricity. Ella pulled her hand back.

"My name's Ella, and I live there."

She pointed to her apartment.

"With my mummy. She does web design," she added proudly, then added, "I'm ten."

Liz nodded but did not take the bait. Instead, the gray-clad girl gazed at the apartment door for a moment, then looked back at Ella. Liz's eyes were very dark, and Ella thought they were rather beautiful. But she felt sudden impatience, a familiar urge to run out in the sunlight and lose herself among the trees.

"Well," Ella said, in her most polite voice, "it's been very nice to meet you, but I must go now."

Ella set off down the stairs and felt, rather than saw or heard, Liz following her. Again, there was a slight whiff of cold air, and Ella shuddered. She was glad when she reached the foyer and saw the caretaker. He was fiddling with the automatic doors, which had never worked properly since Ella had moved in.

"Hello, Declan!" she shouted, almost skipping up to him until she remembered she was too old to act like that. "Have you fixed them?"

"Nah," shrugged the Irishman, scratching his bushy beard. "I think they're another thing that's permanently buggered—I mean, broken. And don't tell your ma I said buggered."

Ella laughed, then glanced around. Liz had gone. There was no sign of the teenage girl anywhere in the foyer. Yet, she had seemed to be right behind Ella a moment earlier.

"What's up, El?" Declan asked, replacing a screwdriver on his tool belt. "You lost something?"

"No," Ella replied. "I just—do you know Liz? I think she lives upstairs somewhere?"

Declan thought for a moment, then shook his head.

"She might just be visiting relatives? This a girl of your age?"

Ella shook her head.

"She's older, I don't know anything about her."

They chatted for a few minutes, then Kate Bewick appeared and asked Declan to come to her office. Kate was obviously busy and looked a bit annoyed to see the caretaker talking to Ella. Remembering her mother's warning, she said a polite goodbye and went outside. Soon she was running into the woods, sending the flock of rooks spiraling up into the air, cawing in disapproval.

***

"Just the one bloke?" asked Declan. "Not a team? That's a bit peculiar, especially from a health and safety perspective."

Kate looked slightly miffed by the question.

"Beggars can't be choosers," she pointed out. "All the local firms have cried off. Most of them say they have too much work on, which is nonsense, given the current economic climate—"

Declan listened as the manager recited the usual litany of problems. He knew that word had gotten out about Rookwood Apartments. It was deemed an unlucky place to work, somewhere that had more than its fair share of accidents. As a result, he feared that the only workmen they would be able to get in the future might be those unable to get hired anywhere else. He tried to put this concern to Kate, but she gave him short shrift.

"This guy is a fully qualified electrician," she insisted. "He's offered to check out the wiring in the East Wing, at no charge, and let us know exactly what needs to be fixed."

Too good to be true, Declan thought. *Or am I being cynical?*

"Sounds like a paragon," he said. "Is he in there now?"

"Yes, he wanted to get started straight away," Kate said. "Want to come and see?"

Declan did not want to see anything in the unoccupied wing. He was just superstitious enough to believe that some places were plagued by misfortune. The East Wing, he felt sure, was jinxed in some way. He preferred not to think about the issue more deeply.

And it's got nothing to do with my own issues, he told himself, as he followed Kate out of the manager's office. *That's just paranoia. I sometimes see things because I feel guilty, frightened. That's all there is to it.*

The electrician, it turned out, was a thirty-something English guy with a neatly groomed goatee, and a somewhat arrogant manner. Declan shook his hand, noting the slightly too-firm grip, an attempt to assert dominance. He returned the pressure, with interest. The man also had a low blink rate, which Declan had seen before in troubling circumstances. He held the man's gaze for a second longer than normal, and the stranger looked away.

Don't read too much into this, Declan thought. *He might just be a bit of a dickhead, no big deal.*

Kate was apparently quite taken with the newcomer, so much so that Declan wondered if she had the hots for the guy. He pushed the thought aside, tried to concentrate on what the electrician was actually saying. Soon, he had reluctantly concluded that the guy did know his trade.

"So, Declan," enthused Kate, after they finished their walkaround, "it's lucky that Jeff here called me on spec, isn't it?"

"It certainly looks like it," Declan responded, trying to sound upbeat.

The caretaker left Kate talking to her new favorite. He felt sour and uneasy about the newcomer. He reasoned that Jeff was probably all right, just a bit too fond of himself. As he walked back alone into the main block, he felt a slight tingling of the spine, a sense of being watched from behind. Then the small, inner voice spoke.

He might be one of them. He could be here to get you.

"Balls!" he snarled at the empty corridor.

Maybe he isn't, maybe it's all perfectly innocent. But maybe the first you'll know about it is from a bullet in the back of the head.

By the time he got back to his office, he was almost running.

***

After fast-forwarding through most of a lousy movie, Paul gave up. He went back to his desk and opened his laptop. Again, he was confronted by the botched attempt at a research paper. He closed the file and checked his email. There was a message from Mari, asking him how he was 'bearing up', offering to 'meet for a coffee'. He almost deleted it, then flagged it for follow up.

Sure, he thought, *we can be jolly good friends now. Like sensible adults, no need for any more heartache.*

Painful memories of the breakup with Mari prompted uncomfortable thoughts of Liz. He had not seen the girl since the night he had moved in. Paul had no idea what he would say to her if they did meet again.

Hi, did we have sex while I was drunk? I kinda think we didn't but just thought I'd check. Oh, we didn't? Great, care for a coffee sometime?

Groaning to himself, he clicked on some sites he used for his work. He had lately been trying to draw parallels between British and American social history. There were definitely some big gaps in his knowledge of Britain, despite having lived in the country for nearly eight years. He had begun to suspect this weakness was holding him back, restricting the range of teaching and research he could do.

"M'kay," he said to himself. "Fifties popular culture. Nice and easy for a Monday evening."

Soon he was reading about a Britain where Winston Churchill was still prime minister, the Cold War was a new peril, and 'flying saucers' were making the headlines. He found himself becoming more absorbed in detail as he explored the early nineteen-fifties. He saw a picture of a strikingly young Queen Elizabeth, white-gloved and waving to crowds from a balcony at Buckingham Palace.

"Bit outside my field, though," he muttered.

He was about to click on another web page when something caught his eye. The article he had skimmed concerned the so-called 'new Elizabethan Era' that people expected when King George the Sixth was succeeded by his daughter. Most of it concerned national self-confidence, largely misplaced, about new British achievements such as the Comet, the first jet airliner. Television was another novelty, and the article went into some detail about how it replaced radio during the Fifties. Paul stared at one particular sentence, which seemed to have some special significance.

Ownership of television sets in Britain soared in

1953, the year of the coronation of the young Queen Elizabeth the second...

He leaned back, closed his eyes. Why did the sentence seem familiar? Had someone at college been talking about it? Or had he read it in an article? His frustration grew, but he knew that trying to force the memory to the surface would only make it worse. He got up and got a soda from the kitchen, then took a gulp while looking out at the view. He glimpsed Ella running around the West Wing, vanishing from sight. Paul smiled, wishing he could still summon up that much energy.

God, he told himself, *you're thirty-six, not sixty-three. Still young.*

Suddenly the memory he had been searching for appeared, startling him with its clarity. Liz had said something about people buying TV sets due to something linked to the Queen. Who had been crowned in 1953. Paul wondered if he had misremembered the conversation.

Can I trust my memory? I've been seeing things, after all.

He thought uneasily of the hallucination he had experienced in the East Wing, the vision of the short, bespectacled doctor. This, in turn, recalled the strange graffiti above the doorway. He had already Googled it and found nothing that suggested a link to Rookwood. However, the scrawled message kept resurfacing.

Another distraction from my actual work, he thought. *I need to get it together.*

Feeling a little stir-crazy, Paul decided to get out into the fresh air. He put on his running gear and resolved to circle the grounds, a distance of about a mile. Soon, he was pounding along one of the pathways that led across the grounds of Rookwood, smiling and waving at a few other residents. Nobody, he noticed, was jogging. One middle-aged couple seemed to be having a picnic. It was all very civilized, and he began to feel more positive as the effects of exercise took hold.

As Paul passed the open gates, he noticed the now-familiar gray-haired woman standing on the pavement opposite. She caught his eye and turned to walk away. He had seen her a couple of times since moving in and reached the tentative conclusion that she was a local with some kind of gripe about Rookwood. The most likely explanation was it increased traffic in this leafy suburb. British people, he had noticed, complained a lot.

Like people anywhere, I guess, he thought.

Paul turned back towards the main building, passing a section of wall that looked like it had been badly repaired at some point. This made him wonder whether the East Wing would ever be finished. He felt uneasy about going near it again but felt ashamed of his anxiety.

Face your fear, he told himself. *Stop avoiding it.*

As he approached the East Wing, he saw a figure moving behind one of the plastic sheets. Paul's heart began to thump. His mouth grew dry. But he kept going, reasoning that it might simply be Declan. Then, as he got closer, he saw that it was a stranger, one in workman's clothes.

Always a rational explanation, he thought.

As Paul ran off the turf and onto the gravel pathway the sound made the stranger turn and look. Paul waved, and the man waved back before moving off into the dim-lit interior.

***

Jeff Bowman waited until the jogger had gone by, then moved to the window again. He had seen Ella running across the lawn toward the woods. That meant Neve was alone in her apartment. He felt a sudden urge to go up there, confront her, impose his will on the woman. On *his* woman. Jeff had to stop himself from doing it, knowing it would be risky. She had called the police on him before. No charges had been brought, of course. It was just one of her ploys, a way to make him look small, weak.

The games these silly bitches play, he thought. *And yet, they can't do without us. Look at this place. No way she can afford to live here, not with a kiddy to raise. She'll welcome me back if I time it right. The breadwinner. The man of the house.*

Jeff looked around at the half-finished walls and ceiling. He had no intention of actually working at Rookwood, it would be far too big a job for two guys, never mind one. It had been far easier to get in than he had feared. All he had to do now, after making a show of assessing the problem, was submit a quote for the work. He would make it so low Kate Bewick would jump at it. Jeff could tell the manager was desperate to get the job finished.

Another woman trying to do a man's job and obviously floundering, he thought. *God, when will this feminist lunacy end?*

Something fell, a loud crash from the corridor, or maybe a neighboring room. Jeff held his breath for a moment, then relaxed. He had been jumpy since arriving and would be glad to get out of the East Wing. But he had to pretend to do a thorough check. He made some notes on his tablet computer, nothing fancy, but enough to fool a non-expert. Then, when he had Kate's permission to be at Rookwood, he could keep an eye on his girlfriend and their child. For a while. So he could plan the next stage.

They'll stop you.

The thought, profoundly unwelcome, took him by surprise. Jeff was used to being in control, setting boundaries, even in his own mind. Self-doubt was one obvious mark of a weakling. Yet as soon as he dismissed the first troubling notion, another one arose. And another.

You'll fail. You'll look weak and stupid. She'll humiliate you. The kid will see you, emasculated.

"No!" he exclaimed, and his voice echoed in the empty room. "No, that's garbage. I just need to plan this carefully before I make my move."

You're scared. You don't really know what to do. Spineless.

Jeff shook his head, cursing loudly now. He felt rising anger, directionless, chaotic. But then he noticed something else, along with the infuriating, belittling thoughts. The room seemed to be growing darker and the air colder. Hairs rose on the back of his neck, and he spun around, sure there was someone behind him. There was nobody there.

But there is somebody here, came the sneering thought. *A gutless wonder called Jeff.*

"Shut up!" he shouted.

Jeff started to walk across the room, heading for an external doorway. But when he tried to push out through the plastic sheeting, it seemed to wrap itself around him. A gust of wind must have struck the side of the building then, because Jeff was shoved back into the room. And now he was not alone. Shadowy figures, their faces blurred, clustered around him. They were whispering, discussing him, commenting on his weakness, his failure.

"He needs to man up. He needs to do something. He needs to take back control of his life."

For a moment, he felt terror. But then the phantoms came closer, and he felt their thoughts merging with his. It became impossible to tell where Jeff ended and the cold, nebulous strangers began. Into his mind seeped visions of what he might do, what he could do, what he should do. Where he had felt doubt, now he experienced an icy clarity.

"Yes," he said, as the whisperers swirled around him. "Yes, I see it now. She needs to be taught a lesson."

***

Ella kept a record of her discoveries in a small notebook. A few months earlier she had seen a TV documentary about Charles Darwin and decided that, like him, she would note everything down. This evening in Rookwood she had spotted several varieties of beetle, plus earwigs, centipedes, and a really huge spider. She felt frustrated at not being able to take pictures of any of them to identify their species and made a note about that, too.

ASK MUMMY FOR PHONE SO I CAN IDENTIFY INSECTS

She underlined the sentence twice, then closed her spiral-bound notebook. She stood up and looked around. Shadows raced across the grass, climbed the front of Rookwood. The sun was obscured by big, dark clouds that threatened rain. Ella decided to go in rather than risk getting wet.

That's sensible behavior, she thought, as she picked her way out of the wood. *Mummy will be pleased with me. I can ask for ice cream.*

The American man who lived on the floor above Ella was jogging around the West Wing, heading back to the entrance. He waved at her, and she waved back. Just because her mother did not like someone did not mean Ella had to shun them. Besides, he seemed lonely.

As Ella walked into the foyer there was a rumble of thunder, followed by a downpour. Rain bounced on the pathway outside and drummed loudly on the windows. The doors of the elevator that was still working were just closing on the American. Ella ran up the stairs, anticipating ice cream, planning out the next phase in her campaign to obtain a phone.

"Something bad might happen."

Liz was standing at the top of the stairs, between Ella and her apartment. The girl was looking down at Ella.

"What do you mean?" Ella asked. "What's wrong?"

Liz stepped back, around the corner, so that she was out of sight. It was an odd thing to do, and Ella advanced cautiously up the last few steps, peeped around the corner. Liz was gone. Ella wondered how the teenager had disappeared. Then she heard someone coming up the stairs behind her.

"Hello, Ella."

She recognized the voice at once, but before she could run a hand seized her by the arm.

"Now," said Jeff, "it's not polite to ignore people. Hello, Ella!"

His grip grew tighter, painful.

"You're hurting me!" Ella cried.

Jeff grinned down at her, and for a moment Ella thought she saw another face somehow blended with his, a masked face with strange, gleaming eyes.

"I know," he said, and shoved her across the hallway, toward the apartment door.

***

Paul crossed to his apartment from the elevator and paused as he unlocked the door. He thought he heard raised voices, maybe coming up the stairwell. He concluded that maybe somebody had their TV turned up loud and had perhaps left their door open.

Once inside, he grabbed a soda and started to undress, planning to take a shower after his run. He felt better, more upbeat, almost daring depression to try and claim him now. He sauntered over to the half-open window to look out at the city. The rain falling on Rookwood had not yet reached Tynecastle, which was still bathed in golden, evening sunlight. Again, voices came from somewhere below, and along with them a dull thud, as if something had fallen. Or someone.

Not a TV, he thought, feeling uneasy. Something happening on the floor below.

There was a shattering sound, immensely loud in his quiet apartment. He looked down just in time to see a man sailing out into the air in a wide arc. The man was dressed in overalls, flailing his arms as he flew, accompanied by a myriad of glass shards. It looked unreal to Paul, like a clever visual effect in a movie. But there was something grimly final about the crunch of impact as the figure struck the turf. The man lay still, head bent sickeningly under his body, limbs splayed like a ragdoll.

Paul stood frozen, trying to process what he had just seen. Someone was screaming, a woman it sounded like. When the screamer paused for breath Paul heard a child sobbing and thought of Ella. He rushed out and scrambled down the stairs, almost running on the first-floor landing.

"What happened?" gasped the Irishman.

"I dunno," admitted Paul.

The screaming had stopped. When they entered the Cotters' flat, they saw Neve sitting on the floor, in a corner by the window. The glass had been shattered and the curtains were billowing inward. Rain was already darkening the edge of a white rug. Ella was standing, looking out at the storm, crying more quietly now.

Declan rushed over to Neve, asking her if she was all right. The woman looked up, seemed not to recognize the Irishman. Feeling awkward, an intruder rather than a helper, Paul walked around Ella until he could hunker down and look her in the face.

"What happened, honey?" he asked.

Ella reached up and wiped her nose with the sleeve of her shirt. Then she looked Paul in the eye and spoke.

"Liz stopped the bad men."

Chapter 6

"How wide would you say the gravel driveway was, sir?" asked Detective Sergeant Farson.

Paul shrugged irritably, not seeing the point of the question. Farson had gone over his statement several times already, apparently not satisfied with some of its aspects. Paul was still shocked by the violent death he had witnessed. They were standing in his apartment, looking out at the scene below. The body had just been bagged up and taken off in an ambulance. Now, Paul could see a uniformed officer recovering and bagging fragments of glass.

"I don't know," he answered. "It's about ten feet wide, something like that. Why?"

Farson opened Paul's window a little wider, gestured down at the damp turf. The rain had stopped a few minutes earlier. The contorted outline of the body was clearly discernible.

"Jeff Bowman landed on the grass, not the gravel," he said. "Which means we can reasonably conclude he didn't fall out of the window, nor was he simply pushed. No, he was hurled, thrown, flung. Doesn't that strike you as a little—peculiar?"

Paul stared at the detective, then joined him at the window. Farson was right. It had been right in front of Paul but had not registered properly, presumably thanks to the mental trauma.

"You're right," he said, wonderingly. "The guy flew out there, he didn't just fall. Like he'd been shot from a catapult. Jesus!"

Farson snapped his black notebook closed, slipped it back into his pocket.

"Yes, sir," he said evenly. "And the only other people in the room were one frightened woman, and an even more frightened ten-year-old girl. No sign of the Incredible Hulk or similar characters. So officially, it's an annoying detail we can't really explain and will, therefore, play down."

Paul felt confused.

"Will you classify it as an accident, then?"

"I won't classify it as anything," Farson said briskly. "Not my job, I just gather facts and interview witnesses. But the guy attacked his former partner and her daughter—that much is undoubtedly true. It could be argued that he fell out of the window in a struggle. Which is plausible if you're not actually looking at the scene. If I were a gambling man, I'd put money on the coroner reaching that conclusion."

Paul nodded, still confused.

"That's all for now, Mister Mahan," said Farson. "I'll be in touch if we need to talk to you again."

Paul nodded, walked the officer over to the door. As Farson stepped out into the hallway he stopped, turned, and raised an eyebrow.

"Oh, just one more thing," he said. "Did the little girl say anything to you? When you entered the flat?"

Paul hesitated, and Farson reached into his lightweight jacket, took out his notebook again.

"I think she said something about—about a bad man," Paul said finally. "I can't be sure."

Farson held his notebook for a moment without opening it, then put it away again. He smiled, nodded.

"This is a weird one, isn't it?"

Before Paul could think of a reply, the detective headed down the stairs. Back inside his apartment, Paul watched as a cab drew up outside the police perimeter. Neve Cotter appeared, weighted with baggage, followed by Ella, then by Declan Mooney carrying more bags. The little girl looked up as the cab driver helped stow their things in the trunk. Ella gave a little wave, and Paul raised his hand in farewell. He knew the Cotters were going to stay with Neve's mother, ostensibly until the smashed window was fixed. But he wondered if they would ever be back.

Should I move out? But where would I go? Back to Mike's?

He ruled out leaving for now and tried to make sense of what Ella had said to him. On the face of it, it was crazy. Liz had not been in the apartment, and even if she had been, a teenage girl could not throw a grown man out of a window. Paul had not been wholly honest with Farson because he did not want to appear crazy or subject Ella to any more police attention.

Maybe she imagined Liz somehow rescuing her? Kids have made up weirder things. But why?

Suspicions about what Liz might be had grown impossible to ignore. Paul did not believe in ghosts. But when he pondered his experiences since moving in, he found he was afraid of them, despite his disbelief. Yet, Liz had seemed as real as anyone else. Merely a strange human being, not a conventional idea of a spook.

A ghost that puts a drunken academic to bed, he thought. *British tabloids would pay good money for that one.*

Paul closed the window and decided to call Mike. He needed to tell someone, talk through the situation. He hoped that Mike's pragmatic way of thinking would explain it all away, make sense of his strange experiences. But then it occurred to him that talking on the phone was not the best way to discuss whatever might be happening at Rookwood. He texted Mike instead, suggesting they 'talk over some stuff' at work the next day.

He had just sent the text when there was a loud rap at the door. His heart fluttered for a moment at the thought that it might be Liz. But when he checked, the distorted view through the peephole showed the face of Sadie Prescott. Paul opened the door, wondering what the head of the Tenants Association might want. He hoped she would not ask for a subscription.

"Doctor Mahan, I wonder if I could have a word?"

Paul gestured her to come in. He soon discovered that Mrs. Prescott's idea of 'a word' was a continuous barrage of talk, delivered in a voice used to addressing meetings. The gist of her monologue was that People Were Concerned, and Something Must Be Done. Paul took advantage of a pause to offer her a seat and a cup of tea.

"No time, no time, but thank you!" she exclaimed. "I'm too busy trying to coordinate our response to the phenomena."

"Phenomena?" Paul asked.

The woman made a sweeping gesture that seemed to embrace the building, the grounds, and Paul himself.

"The haunting, Doctor Mahan," she said, in a stage whisper. "The psychic forces besieging us."

When he did not respond, she proceeded to explain just what response she had in mind. Paul felt his heart sink as Sadie Prescott outlined her plans. He felt even worse when she asked if he was prepared to take part.

***

"So, what's this about?" asked Mike Bryson, slumping into the chair facing Paul.

"It's complicated," Paul replied.

Mike rolled his eyes, looked around Paul's cramped office.

"You do have a way of making things more complicated than they need to be," the Englishman observed. "Can you sum it up in a few words?"

Paul took a breath, bracing himself for his friend's reaction.

"My apartment building might be haunted."

Mike looked at Paul for a moment, then nodded.

"Okay, now can you sum it up for me in a lot more words?"

Ten minutes later, Mike emitted a low whistle.

"Either you've actually gone bonkers, which seems unlikely as you're so dull in other respects," said the Englishman. "Or there really is something paranormal going on. I mean, I read about the drill incident, and then this guy going out of the window. But I never realized things were so—well, strange."

Mike got up and started to pace back and forth, a mannerism Paul recognized as part of his friend's lecturing style. He smiled to himself, despite his anxiety, knowing Mike had at least got his brain in gear.

"Okay, you think this Liz might be an actual ghost," Mike said. "And that she threw this unpleasant bloke, Bowman, out of the window?"

Paul shrugged.

"That's what the little girl said, or implied."

Mike stopped pacing and darted a finger at Mike.

"She said, according to you, Liz stopped the bad men. Not bad man, singular."

Paul made a helpless gesture, did not bother to reply. Mike resumed his pacing.

"You felt some kind of presence in the East Wing," he said. "More than one entity?"

"Could be. I'm a little hazy on that whole incident," Paul admitted. "But it seems like a complicated situation. That's why I wanted to talk it over."

Mike threw himself back into the creaking office chair.

"I'm not exactly an expert on actual ghosts," the Englishman admitted. "Sure, I teach students about Gothic horror, but you seem to be living it. What you need is an expert. I suppose you could always try Rodria."

The name was vaguely familiar to Paul. He recalled some kind of scandal a few years earlier but could not remember the details.

"Max Rodria?" Mike went on. "Paranormal researcher, works in the physics department. Allegedly. He seems to spend a lot of time publicizing his research, a lot less time actually doing it."

They discussed Rodria, whom Mike disliked for his egotism, while admitting that 'scientific ghost-hunters are thin on the ground'. Eventually, as they ran out of time, Paul agreed to approach the physicist, as it could do no harm. The friends parted with promises to meet up for a drink. After Mike had left, Paul looked up Rodria on the university's intranet and sent him a carefully worded message.

***

"What is it with you and the cops, Dec?"

The question came out of nowhere and left Declan floundering to respond. He started to say he had no problem with the police, and Kate was just stereotyping him as a shifty Irishman. But the manager, standing over him in his small office, cut him off with an impatient shake of her head.

"Come on, Dec," Kate said, leaning up against his desk. "We've known each other a while now. The police really put the wind up you, I can see it in your face. If there's something that could bite me in the arse, I need to know."

"Oh, I might have known it was your precious career you were worried about," he said, with sudden anger.

"Hurt your feelings?" Kate asked, in a wheedling voice. "Come on, we're both grownups. What is it? Seriously?"

Declan sighed, found himself scratching the back of his right hand, then saw Kate watching him do it.

"The tattoo you had removed," she said. "Paramilitary, right? It can only be that, or something you regretted when you sobered up, like 'I Love Gary Barlow.'"

Declan had to laugh, despite the tension. He decided to tell Kate some of the story, just enough to satisfy her and stop her from digging further.

"I was a stupid fourteen-year-old," he said. "My big brother, my uncles, they were all in—call it the organization. The tattoo was bravado, showing that I didn't care who knew what side I was on."

Kate nodded, face serious again. Declan resisted the temptation to look her in the eye for too long, knowing that was the mark of a liar, and suspecting she would know it too.

Everyone watches true crime documentaries these days.

"At first, it was just keeping a lookout for the cops on the street corner, that sort of thing," he continued. "But then, when I left school, they got me hiding guns in the attic, lying to my mother about it. I know for a fact one of those rifles was used to kill a lad not much older than me. This was all a good few years ago, of course. Before the ceasefire, and the treaty."

"So you got out," Kate said quietly.

"Right," he said. "I got out of Ireland when I could, kicked around Scotland, then England, places where your religion doesn't matter, where politics isn't life or death. I learned to fix things, I was always good with my hands. And I ended up here. Thing is, I don't know if the police are looking for me or not. I was just raised to be scared of them, you know?"

Kate looked at Declan for a few seconds, then stood up and laid a hand on his shoulder.

"You should have told me, Dec. I would never have held it against you. We all do stupid things when we're young."

After she had gone, Declan felt sick. He rushed along the corridor to the washroom and threw up into a basin, then studied his pale, sweaty face in the mirror. His eyes were bloodshot from lack of sleep, his beard unkempt, his not-quite-bald head in need of a razor.

Something moved in one of the cubicles behind him, thumping against a wooden door. Declan froze, stared into the reflection of the row of doors. Three were open, one was closed, the one on the far left. Again, the noise came, a little louder this time, suggesting a weighty object tapping on the inside of the door.

Then came a click. It was a familiar sound, one Declan hated. Whenever it happened in a movie or TV show, he switched off or changed the channel. It was the sound of a pistol being cocked. A gun being prepared to fire.

"Declan."

He straightened up, still unable to turn, terror making his limbs feel heavy as lead. The voice had spoken in an intense whisper. Its accent was like his own, Northern Irish, but thicker, harsher. Declan knew, if he had the courage to look, he would see a figure in combats with a balaclava covering its face, except for the eyes and a slit for the mouth. The mouth would be open in a humorless grin, revealing yellowed, uneven teeth.

"Declan, boy, there's only one punishment for informers. You know what it is."

"No, please!" Declan cried, finally turning to face the masked figure. "I didn't mean to hurt anybody, I just wanted out, and they offered me a chance to get away—"

"Good men shot down like dogs, Declan. Because you told the fekkin' British where they'd be."

The arm holding the pistol swung up, the blue-black muzzle aimed low. Declan put his hands together, praying for the first time in many years, whimpering for mercy. He called upon a God he had often doubted. The mouth of the stranger smiled its yellow smile, and a gloved finger squeezed the trigger.

The gunshot was deafening in the enclosed space, but Declan hardly noticed it. He was too busy clutching his knee, writhing on the avocado-colored tiles. Blood spurted through his fingers, and he could feel the kneecap in fragments, sharp edges of bone just under the taut skin.

Declan howled in pain and fear, squeezed his eyes shut, and waited for the second bullet.

***

"I'm surprised it took you so long, Mahan," rumbled Max Rodria. "I've been following this little debacle with considerable interest. The place has a murky history, though the clowns in our local press seem largely ignorant of it."

The scientist stood up, extended a meaty hand that Paul shook, somewhat reluctantly. Rodria was in his mid-forties, Paul knew, but the man looked older, in part because the physicist was borderline obese. He cut an imposing figure, though, at a shade over six feet. Rodria carefully cultivated the image of an eccentric British professor, dressing in tweeds with elbow patches. His desk was covered in papers, journals, and dog-eared books, adding to the image of an academic in a movie rather than real life.

"Do take a pew, old chap," Rodria went on. "And unburden yourself. I'm sure you have an interesting tale to tell."

"Okay," Paul said, uncomfortably, "you know there have been some weird happenings at Rookwood. What you don't know is that—I think I've encountered some kind of presence. Well, at least two presences. By which I mean ghosts, I guess."

Rodria took out an ornate pipe, which he was not allowed to smoke on college premises. Instead, he sat sucking the stem and nodding as Paul gave his account of his encounter with Liz, then his vision of the doctor in the East Wing. Rodria interrupted a couple of times, asking for more detail. But he seemed oddly dismissive of some facts that Paul saw as significant. The graffiti on the wall did not impress him.

"My dear chap," Rodria scoffed, "any teenager might have scrawled something on wet plaster. And how exactly does it pertain to what has actually happened? Who is Annie? What is her story?"

Paul had to admit that he did not know, and it rankled. He felt sure that there was more to the odd phrase than random vandalism. But rather than quibble, he moved on to the fact that Liz had been seen by both him and Ella Cotter.

"That gives Liz some independent existence, right?" Paul demanded. "She can't be a hallucination if two people see her, especially since I never mentioned her to the kid. And Ella as good as said she threw a fully-grown man out of a window—an illusion can't do that."

Rodria sucked his pipe, smiled in a self-satisfied way. Paul felt a twinge of sympathy for the man's students. He could guess what was coming. Rodria was, according to Mike, 'terminally addicted to telling the world just how brilliant he is.'

"I have been investigating so-called psychic phenomena for nearly twenty years now," Rodria began. "And I have never encountered any so-called poltergeist activity that could not be explained as a hoax, or misidentification of a natural phenomenon. A man fell out of a window, police say it was the result of a struggle."

Paul began to protest. But Rodria, frowning, held up his pipe for silence.

"Please, let me finish! You came to me for expert advice, after all. Now, the other unpleasant incident was apparently caused by some kind of attack by a young man who seems, if reports are to be believed, to have some mental health issues. He hears voices, according to press reports. In that case, I think we may have something like a parapsychological cause of the young man's behavior. The secret is not in so-called ghosts, but in the building itself."

Rodria heaved himself up out of his chair again and laid a hand on the wall behind his desk. He looked at Paul as if he expected the American to understand something significant. When it became apparent that his student was not going to get it, Rodria heaved a dramatic sigh.

"The fabric of the structure, Paul! Why do you think we always talk about haunted houses, or other sites to which ghosts seem to be confined? Why should ghosts not be free to roam as freely as the living, if they are the spirits of the departed? This can be explained by the concept of place memory. You've not come across it?"

Paul admitted that he had not, and again felt annoyance. He sensed that Rodria was simply rehearsing a talk he had given many times, rather than considering the specific case of Rookwood.

"I've not delved into the paranormal, at least not in real life," Paul said. "I've seen a bunch of horror movies down the years, but I'm guessing they're all wrong?"

Rodria snorted, flopped his corpulent form back into his chair.

"As I said," the scientist rumbled complacently, "popular ideas of ghosts are unscientific. What people call a haunting has rightly been described as a 'stone tape'. It is some kind of residual electromagnetic energy, past events recorded in the fabric of the building, replaying themselves in the minds of the susceptible."

"That doesn't cover what I actually experienced," Paul objected, only for Rodria to give another dismissive wave.

"My dear chap," said the scientist, "what you imagine you experienced—a conversation with a ghost—was simply your brain making sense of this replay I mentioned."

Rodria rose to his feet, indicating that the interview was at an end.

"One thing is certain," he said. "Whatever is manifesting itself at Rookwood is not in any sense alive. It cannot learn, or think, or feel."

***

"Dec, what the hell happened?"

Declan opened his eyes to see Kate's kitten-heeled shoes. Then her face appeared as she knelt by him on the washroom floor.

"What's wrong?" she asked, eyes wide with concern. "Should I call an ambulance?"

"No!" he said instinctively, then realized how absurd the response was. He could still feel the warmth of blood, oozing through the knee of his overall. He did not dare look at the damage. He remembered his boyhood in Belfast, seeing men on crutches, being told they had been 'kneecapped' for being informers. He imagined himself a cripple, unable to work, and moaned in despair.

"Dec, is it your leg?" Kate asked, sounding puzzled now.

He stared at the woman, wondering if she had gone mad. How could she not see the horrific wound, the impact point of a crosscut nine-millimeter round? Then he felt Kate's hand on his, gently unclasping his fingers. He looked down to see his overall unstained, not a trace of blood anywhere. The pain that had been so real a moment before had vanished. Gasping in astonishment, he ran his fingertips over his kneecap, felt nothing but a familiar, intact disc of bone.

But I was shot. I heard the gun, I felt the bullet, he thought. *I can't have just imagined it all.*

"This is getting out of hand," said Kate, helping him to his feet. "You're clearly more than a bit jumpy, Dec. You need to tell me what's going on with you. And how it relates to this place. We can't have you coming unspooled, can we?"

Declan began to stammer out a few words, but Kate shushed him and insisted they go to her office for 'coffee and a bit of sanity'. However, as they left the washroom, Sadie Prescott's voice echoed down the hallway. Kate, sighing, whispered to Declan that they would 'talk this over later, definitely'. Then Mrs. Prescott was upon them, outlining her plans. When Declan made to walk off, the formidable woman insisted that her 'spiritual cleansing' concerned him, too.

"People have seen things, heard things," Mrs. Prescott continued. "Clearly there are disturbed spirits. This place was once a madhouse, after all. And it burned down, killing dozens of staff and patients. That's hardly conducive to a good atmosphere."

Declan could tell that Kate was struggling to maintain her professional demeanor.

"Sadie," the manager said, "we've had some unfortunate accidents, and I don't think a stunt involving some kind of stage performer—"

Soon the two women were openly arguing, with Declan feeling he should intervene on his boss' behalf. But he was still too shaken to do more than murmur a few words of support. Sadie Prescott brushed off all protests and continued to insist that the building needed to be cleansed.

"It's too late to change the arrangements, anyhow," the woman added. "Imelda Troubridge is coming."

"Isn't she that mad woman off the telly?" Declan blurted out.

Sadie Prescott looked at him coldly and took a deep breath.

***

"Imelda Troubridge?" erupted Rodria. "Why didn't you tell me this in the first place?"

Paul shrugged, secretly pleased that he had upset the man.

"It didn't seem important," he admitted. "It's an idea from the chair of the Tenants Association. She thinks a psychic might somehow reveal the nature of the problem. I take it that you don't agree?"

Rodria was becoming red in the face.

"Psychics?" he bellowed. "They're all bloody fakes, and Imelda Troubridge is one of the most ridiculous. She performs in theatres, telling gullible people she's receiving messages from their deceased relatives and pets. She's a tabloid celebrity!"

Paul could not resist a smile.

"Sounds like you two have some previous," he remarked. "What happened?"

"Never mind all that!" retorted Rodria. "If that woman is involved, I don't want to be. Charlatans who claim to speak to the dead do not concern me. When the sideshow is over, by all means, get back in touch. In the meantime, I will bid you good day."

Jesus, thought Paul, as he left Rodria's office, *and he talks about other people putting on an act.*

His encounter with the paranormal researcher seemed to have been futile. Rodria's explanation for the haunting of Rookwood made little sense. When Paul returned to his apartment that evening, he began to seriously consider simply moving out. He checked a few property websites, looking for cheap rentals in or around Tynecastle. It became obvious that his perception of cheap was out of step with economic reality. Financially, Rookwood was the only place he could afford that was not pretty near to being a slum.

"Crap," he moaned, closing various windows.

"You seem upset," said Liz, putting two slender hands on his shoulders.

Paul jumped. Liz giggled, and again he was reminded of how immature she seemed. He moved away from her. Liz looked up at him, her smile fading, dark eyes inscrutable.

"What is it?" she asked. "Aren't you glad to see me? I thought we were friends, Paul."

"Sure," he said, then reconsidered. "Well, kind of. Thing is, there's—there's a problem. A whole lot of problems, in fact."

Liz walked a couple of steps closer. Paul retreated, collided with his bookcase. A heavy volume fell to the floor. Instinctively, he bent down to retrieve it. But before he could pick up the book, Liz had moved swiftly to replace it on the shelf. He felt a slight disturbance of air as she moved by him.

She's as real as I am, he thought. *She can't be a ghost.*

And yet when Liz reached up to touch his cheek, he flinched from contact. She stood motionless, hand raised, then sighed.

"You're scared of me, now," she said accusingly. "People have been telling you lies about me. Or you've been imagining things."

"What happened to Jeff Bowman?" he blurted out. "Did you kill him?"

Liz looked disappointed, made a little pouting mouth.

"Men who hurt little girls, who hurt women—I don't like them," she said simply. "And sometimes I do get a bit carried away. I pushed him, and he fell. Sort of. I haven't been so angry in—well, ages."

"Since you came to Rookwood, maybe?" Paul asked, wondering if she would reveal something more about herself. "When would that have been?"

"Why are you trying to get me to talk about myself?" she asked. "You're much more interesting, Paul. I want to know you better. You seem kind. But a little sad. Lonely."

"What are you?" he demanded. "Because no way are you a regular British teenager, or anything like one."

Liz shrugged, a deliberately cute gesture. But for Paul, it did not quite come off. There was now a distinct chill in the room. He thought ruefully of how Rodria would have to eat his pompous words if he had simply come back here, as Paul had wanted.

"I'm just me," she said finally. "Take me or leave me."

She took a step forward and again he retreated, scrambling clumsily alongside the bookcase until he reached the window. It suddenly occurred to Paul that he, too, might be hurled out into the summer air. Liz stood regarding him for a moment, and then seemed to shimmer and fade. There was a juddering noise, and the window rattled as a strong vibration ran through the walls and floor.

Poltergeist, he thought. *Is that what she is? Or part of it, at least?*

"You're not being very nice, Paul," Liz said plaintively. "If you don't like me, then I won't stay. But I'll be back."

For a split second, he could see the door of the living room through Liz, then he was alone in the apartment. The vibration died, but Paul realized that he was quivering. He ran a shaky hand through his hair, half-fell onto his sofa. Thoughts whirled in his head as he tried to make sense of the encounter.

Ghosts are real, I'm not hallucinating, he told himself. *Now, what do I do about it? Run away? I'd despise myself for that.*

Paul thought about Rodria's theory, of the fabric of the building being permeated with the thoughts and emotions of people who had lived and died there. He wondered if, like many clever ideas, there was a kernel of truth in it. Perhaps ghosts were bound to the same place, but not as simple recordings, as Rodria arrogantly believed.

More like inmates, prisoners, he thought. *Trapped thanks to an unnatural death. Unquiet souls, maybe.*

Paul thought of his own mother, and wondered if her suffering and confusion lived on, in some form, in a New York State mental institution. He could do nothing to help her, at least not now. But perhaps he could do something to dispel the pall of misery and violence that clearly beset Rookwood. For the first time, he might be able to face his own fear, the ever-present dread of ending up like his mother.

Help others, and so help myself, he thought. *Okay, it's a cliché. But that doesn't make it wrong.*

After a few moments of thought, he opened his laptop and wrote an email to Max Rodria. Then he read it over, rewrote it so it had a much more obsequious tone, and sent it. He picked up his phone and called Mike to talk over just how they might go about solving the mystery of Rookwood Asylum. His friend was keen to help, but also wary of 'doing anything too daft'.

"They're calling in a professional psychic," Paul said.

Mike sighed.

"Reality TV nonsense. But if you want moral support at the séance, I'll come along. I'll be the one sitting right by the exit."

As always, Mike's cheerful irreverence made Paul feel better. After they finished talking, Paul decided to call Kate.

I can't make this place my special project without her support, he mused. *And if she's willing to let spiritualists into the place, she can hardly object to a resident doing a little research.*

He started to search for her number, but suddenly found himself unable to work his cell phone. He gazed at the device in puzzlement, wondering what to do next. The silence of the apartment closed in around him as he sat, motionless. His mind struggled to make sense of the thing he held, the strange black rectangle with the bright pictures. It was almost magical, like something from another world.

It's like a tiny television set! The sort of thing they might have in the future, when people are living on the Moon.

The puzzling interlude ended as suddenly as it had begun. Normality reasserted itself, and Paul flicked a thumb across the screen to find his contacts list. He dismissed the momentary aberration as a symptom of stress.

CHAPTER 7

"I was a stupid kid," said Declan. "But I sort of knew what I was getting into."

He was sitting opposite Kate in the Grey Horse, a pub just down the road from Rookwood. It was a weekday evening, and the place was half full, reasonably quiet. The clientele seemed to be a mixture of professional types grabbing a meal after work, and younger people just beginning a night out.

"This was in Belfast?" Kate asked.

He nodded, took a swig from his pint of Guinness, wiped the froth from his mouth. Kate waited patiently, and for the first time, Declan felt he could probably trust her. If not with his whole story, then maybe with some of it.

"I got involved with one side in the Troubles, as they called them," he said. "This was in the late Eighties, early Nineties, when things were really bad. I had family involved with the paramilitaries, so I started out as a kind of messenger boy, lookout, that sort of thing."

He took another gulp of stout, wiped his mouth reflexively. Kate produced a small tissue, leaned over, and dabbed some foam away. The gesture surprised him. He mumbled thanks, laughed.

"The curse of the big beard," he said. "Maybe I should switch to wine."

Kate laughed in turn.

"Not your style," she remarked. "But go on, Dec, what happened?"

"I got in too deep," he explained. "I ended up—people got hurt because of what I did, and what I didn't do. I was quite the good little Catholic then. Mass on Sunday, confession, the whole thing. I couldn't reconcile my faith with what I was doing. So I went to the other side for help. I offered them some information, if they could get me out of the bloody mess I was in."

He saw realization dawning on Kate's face as the implications of what he said sank in.

"The other side—you mean MI5, something like that?"

Declan shrugged. He recalled the covert meetings with a succession of hard-faced men whose names were obviously fabricated. A John, a Charlie, a Keith, no last names. He tried to describe the way he had gradually become entangled in the security forces' web, become a British agent before he even knew it.

"And you were still a teenager?" Kate asked, aghast.

He nodded.

"And then the people I was betraying found out," he said simply. "Both sides had their informers, you see. I had to get out. After a lot of moving around, I ended up here."

"And you're afraid of them catching up with you, the terrorists?" Kate asked. "Okay, but why be scared of the police?"

Declan sighed, made a helpless gesture.

"First, because any kind of criminal investigation might generate publicity, and certain people might notice me," he explained. "And second, because there are people embedded in the police who still report back to my old comrades."

Kate nodded, then reached out and put her hand on his. Again, it was a surprisingly tender gesture, and for a moment, he wondered if she had feelings for him. He dismissed the idea as irrelevant.

"But what happened in the washroom?" Kate asked. "That had nothing to do with the police, right?"

Declan tried to explain the sense of menace he had felt since starting at Rookwood. He described the visions he had had, of masked men sent to punish him. It was as if his nightmares had bled over into his waking hours.

"Hallucinations," Kate said. "Surely that's all they were."

"Hallucinations can't smash your kneecap, or make it seem like it's smashed," he retorted. "Sure, maybe it is all in my mind. But if that's so, I'm going barmy, properly insane. And, given all the other things that have happened, how can it all be up here?"

Declan tapped his forehead with an index finger. He noticed Kate looking slightly uncomfortable, and realized he had raised his voice, come close to ranting at her in fact. Some of the talk at nearer tables faltered, creating an awkward silence, before the chatter resumed. Glancing around, Declan wondered what the normal, everyday people talking, drinking, eating, would think of his story.

They'd think I was barmy, he thought ruefully. *And they might be right.*

"Okay," Kate sighed, "I've tried very hard to ignore the weird stuff. Focus on the job, career, all that jazz. But you're right. There's something seriously wrong at Rookwood."

"You think this TV psychic will do any good?" he asked, trying not to sound incredulous.

Kate shrugged.

"Give the people what they want," she said.

Declan groaned quietly.

"I've seen what a lot of people want, believe me," he said, picking up his pint again. "And it can be pretty stupid and dangerous."

Kate was about to speak when her phone rang. She spoke to someone for a few moments, then explained where she and Declan were before ending the call.

"That's our new American tenant," she explained to Declan. "He wants to talk to me about the haunting."

***

Paul set off for the Grey Horse, mulling over what he might say to Kate Bewick and the caretaker. Both must be well aware of the strange situation at Rookwood, he reasoned. And yet, they might not agree that his approach, trying to find the root of the problem, was best.

But I'm a historian, he thought, as he walked down toward the open gates. *Digging into the past is what I do.*

"We must study the past if we're to understand the present," he said under his breath, rehearsing the argument he might have to make.

As he left the bounds of Rookwood, Paul noticed the gray-haired lady he had seen on his first visit. On a sudden impulse he decided to speak to her, reasoning that if she had worked at the old asylum, she might have some useful information. When she saw him approaching, she looked disconcerted and started to hurry away. She took out a remote and unlocked a small, powder blue Fiat.

"Please wait," he called after the woman. "I just want to talk about Rookwood."

The woman paused, hand on the car door. She looked him up and down as he walked up to her, her expression a mixture of worry and suspicion.

"What do you want?" she asked. "It's not a crime to stand on a public street, not in this country anyway."

"I know," he said in a placatory tone, "but you seem to spend a lot of time outside that place."

He nodded at Rookwood, just visible over its surrounding walls.

"What do you want?" she repeated, opening the car door. "If you've got nothing sensible to say, I've got better things to do."

"Did you work there, in the old asylum?" he asked, bluntly. "Because if so, you must know some bad things happened there. Something that left a—a kind of residue."

Now the woman looked genuinely annoyed.

"How dare you?" she demanded. "Do I look that old? Of course, I didn't work there. Nobody who worked there is still alive."

"Because they died in a fire, right?" he asked.

The woman nodded reluctantly.

"And what caused the fire?" Paul went on.

"I don't know!" she replied, sounding exasperated. "I was less than a year old when it happened, young man."

Paul decided to give up. She was clearly not in the mood to volunteer information. But as he turned to walk away, the woman called after him.

"Have you seen—any of them?"

He stopped and turned. The woman was still standing, her expression anxious. He wondered how much she knew about recent events inside Rookwood.

"You mean ghosts?" he asked.

She nodded.

"Yeah," he said. "I've seen a girl called Liz. She's about sixteen, I think. Or was, when she died. And I'm not the only one to see her. There was some kind of doctor as well. Why do you ask?"

Instead of replying, the woman stared at him, her mouth moving silently. Then she climbed into the car, slammed the door, and started the engine. He watched as the Fiat sped off, swerving erratically in the light traffic, and wondered what the woman's deal was.

Too young to work there, he thought. *But maybe her mother or father did. She might be wondering how and why they died.*

He filed the idea away for future reference and resumed his walk to the Grey Horse. Not for the first time, he noticed that his spirits had lifted simply by leaving the environs of Rookwood.

***

Nearly two hours had passed since Paul had met with Kate and Declan. In that time, he had been totally open about his experiences since arriving at Rookwood. He was fairly sure, reading non-verbal signals, that Declan had not been so forthcoming. Kate, for her part, insisted that she had never felt anything more concrete than 'cold spots' and 'a sense of being watched sometimes'.

"I wonder if that's because you're less vulnerable," Paul suggested. "If I have my mother's tendency towards—well, let's call it what it is, mental illness, I might be more susceptible. You might be altogether more well-balanced, Kate—a stable personality, with no dark corners or suppressed traumas."

She laughed at the suggestion, but nervously.

"Yeah, we're talking about a taboo subject," Paul went on. "Not ghosts or hauntings, but lunacy, madness, being crazy—all the usual terms apply. Nobody's comfortable with it. It's so much easier to be afraid of ghosts than of going insane."

"And you think," Declan said slowly, "that Rookwood puts those two fears together, preys on people's mental vulnerability?"

Paul nodded, glad that the caretaker wasn't dismissing his ideas out of hand.

"It does make a kind of sense," he pointed out. "A place where terrible mental torment occurred. What Ella Cotter said about bad men keeps bugging me. Could she have meant the—let's call them ghosts, psychic residue, whatever—were kind of driving Jeff Bowman to commit some heinous crime?"

Kate shook her head, frowning.

"But how does that square with him being flung out of the window?" she asked. "This Liz character you and Ella both encountered seems to have protected the girl."

"Two rival factions," Declan said. "Or rather, rival forces. Liz on the one hand, this doctor you saw on the other."

"Except that Ella said, 'bad *men*,'" Paul pointed out. "That implies some kind of group, perhaps former inmates. Or maybe staff members."

They discussed the possibility for a while but reached no conclusion. However, Kate surprised Paul by giving a possible name to the doctor.

"Miles Rugeley Palmer," she said. "He's listed as the last director of the asylum. He died, along with most of the staff and patients, when it was burned down. When I took the job, I did a little background research, that was one of the details I thought was irrelevant. But the name stuck in my mind—it's rather unusual."

A few seconds of Googling confirmed what Kate had said. Paul noted that the doctor's body had been identified from dental records after the asylum was gutted by fire. He found news reports that stated almost everyone in the building had 'perished from burns or smoke inhalation'. The cause of the fire, however, was apparently never established.

"So that's where you'll start?" Declan asked. "Trying to find out what went on in the run-up to the fire?"

"It seems logical," Paul said. "Even if it was just a horrendous accident, we're still living through a kind of paranormal aftermath. If we're going to do something about it, we have to at least try to understand it."

"But what can we do?" Kate asked. "Exorcise the spirits?"

"Tell Annie's story," Paul said. "How about that? You must have seen those words. Maybe we can identify her. Perhaps simply telling the truth will free the captive spirits, or whatever you want to call them."

Kate and Declan both looked dubious but did not disagree outright. Paul could not blame them for being skeptical. He felt sure that getting at the truth would help in some way.

But maybe that's the professional historian in me, he thought. *Always assuming knowledge confers power.*

"We'd better be getting back," Kate said, checking her watch. "That woman will be here soon."

"What woman?" Paul asked, then realized who she meant.

"Yep," Kate said, seeing his appalled expression. "Imelda Troubridge, famed psychic, is coming to have a look around tonight. Apparently, she was very keen to drop everything and rush up here from Manchester. Her train should be arriving in a few minutes."

Declan gave a contemptuous grunt.

"Yeah, violent death—it brings these publicity seekers buzzing around like flies."

As they walked back to Rookwood, the summer sun began to set, bathing the old asylum in a garish red light.

***

Imelda Troubridge was a short, middle-aged woman wearing a striking amount of jewelry. Every finger was adorned with flashy rings, and her throat and wrists were festooned with a prodigious amount of gold. As she breezed into the foyer of Rookwood, Paul wondered how long it took the alleged psychic to get through airport security. She was also dressed in flowing garments that, to Paul, seemed to be somewhere between a nightdress and a sari. Imelda was accompanied by a stocky, tough-looking man with a camera, who seemed to follow her every tinkling move.

Sadie Prescott was at the head of a small welcoming committee of about a dozen residents, most of whom Paul knew by sight. Before Kate Bewick could say anything, Sadie rushed forward to greet the celebrity.

"We're all so grateful you could come!"

"Ah yes!" Imelda breathed, dramatically. "I already feel turbulence in the mental atmosphere. There are so many troubled souls here."

As her cameraman continued filming, the psychic was introduced to Kate and Declan, then the residents. Paul noticed, as he stayed at the back of the small crowd, that Imelda made a point of holding onto a person's hand a little longer than normal. She also looked people in the eye with a practiced show of sincerity. To him, she reeked of phoniness, like a too-slick politician. But she was clearly more impressive to others.

After the introductions, Imelda asked to be taken to the 'main focus of the disturbance'. This prompted some discussion, as the Cotter's flat was the site of the most recent incident. However, after a couple of minutes it was agreed that the East Wing was, as Declan put it, 'the spookiest part of the building.' As soon as she heard this, the psychic declared that she would 'conduct a preliminary investigation' and swept out of the foyer.

"This is like a cheap sideshow," Paul said to Kate. "How can anyone be taken in by this stuff?"

Kate looked helpless.

"If something serious happens, I could be sacked," she lamented. "But if I'd kept her out, I'd have Sadie making formal complaints to my bosses in London."

"There's a good chance nothing will happen," said Paul, keen to reassure her. "It's not as if she has any special abilities. And these ghosts seem to zero in on individuals who are isolated to some degree, not people in crowds."

By the time Paul and Kate caught up with the main group, Imelda was standing in the middle of the first room. The woman was breathing deeply, eyes closed, hand raised for silence. Her taciturn assistant had turned on his camera light, as the sunlight was almost gone, and the room was deep in shadow. The sky visible through the plastic-covered windows was the color of blood.

"Yes," said Imelda. "Yes! I sense troubled souls, swarming around us, seeking peace, but not finding it. There is no death, merely transition. But sometimes that process is stalled, and spirits that have suffered great trauma linger in the places they knew in, what we call, life."

The medium walked around the room where the drill incident had occurred, making comments that—to Paul—merely proved she could follow news reports. Again, however, her audience seemed impressed. There was rapt silence from the onlookers as Imelda turned slowly in the center of the room, jewelry tinkling.

"Get out!"

A slender figure had appeared in the doorway behind Imelda. There was a scream, gasps, some cursing from Declan. Paul recognized Liz just as she vanished. Imelda herself twisted around in an ungainly fashion, ended up facing an empty doorway.

"Did you get that, Steve?" she asked her cameraman.

The stocky man shook his head. Onlookers scrambled to describe what they had seen, giving a more or less accurate description of Liz.

Paul felt an odd sense of relief. For the first time, multiple eyewitnesses had seen 'his' ghost.

"Who are you?" Imelda asked, gesturing for quiet. "Why do you want me to leave?"

There was a loud bang somewhere nearby. Then a scraping noise, and Paul thought of a desk or some other item of furniture being dragged along a hard floor. The spotlight on Steve's camera flickered. His formerly impassive features looked puzzled and he seemed about to speak to Imelda. She waved a glittering hand at Steve, and he resumed filming.

"What is your name, spirit?" the psychic demanded, raising her voice. "Can you tell us what your name was, here on the earthly plane?"

Silence. Someone coughed. Then another pointed and yelled. Paul noticed it a second later. One of Imelda Troubridge's flamboyant necklaces was being drawn up from behind, tightening around her neck. Steve spotted it at the same moment. Dropping the camera, the man lunged forward and grabbed at the necklaces, started to pull back against the invisible force. Troubridge herself, eyes popping, clutched impotently at her throat.

There was a scrimmage as several people tried to help. Then Steve reeled backward, jerking the psychic off her feet and sending them sprawling to the floor. Whatever had held her necklace had let go. Some people pushed past Paul, heading for the exit. He heard someone else declare that it was 'just part of the act', but not with any great conviction. Kate's voice sounded above the confused hubbub.

"Let's get out of here now, people!" she pleaded. "No shoving, make it nice and orderly."

A couple of minutes later, Imelda was in Kate's office, sipping on a cup of hot tea. Declan had offered to put a slug of whiskey into the beverage, but the psychic insisted that she 'did not pollute her body with stimulants'. "Pity," Declan had replied tersely, earning himself a hard stare from Steve.

Most of the residents had dispersed, evidently believing the show was over, if it had been a show. From what Paul overheard, opinion was divided. But one thing was certain; Imelda Troubridge wanted to 'have another try', as she put it. When Kate, Declan, and Paul all urged her to quit, she grew stubborn.

"I have a duty to troubled souls!" she declared. "I must help them move on."

"Where to, madam, if I might ask?" queried Declan, in a skeptical tone. "Are you talking about heaven here?"

Imelda nodded curtly, her disapproval of the caretaker evident.

"So-called skeptics may mock," she said, "but yes. What some call heaven is a higher plane of existence that we all move on to, eventually. It's up to those who are gifted, like myself, to assist those having difficulty making that adjustment."

Declan snorted, and Paul guessed what the Irishman was going to say next.

"You'll excuse me," Declan went on, "but from what we've seen lately, I'd say a more likely destination for these lost souls is the other place. Down below."

The psychic got unsteadily to her feet, handed her teacup to Kate with a polite 'thank you', then jabbed a finger at Declan.

"There is no Hell, other than the one we make for ourselves on earth, through ignorance and cruelty," she insisted. "This place is, I feel sure, a kind of purgatory for the confused souls. I will return tomorrow morning, and in the light of day, I feel things will be a little—less fraught. For all concerned."

Imelda started to sweep out, but as she jingled past Paul, he laid a hand on her arm.

"Excuse me," he said, "but would you mind checking what your assistant actually got on video? To satisfy our curiosity?"

"Good idea," said Kate quickly. "Don't cameras sometimes pick up things people miss in these situations?"

For a moment, the woman looked as if she would snub the request, but then Paul sensed her reading the room.

"Of course," she said. "Steve, can you connect your camera with Ms. Bewick's computer?"

The assistant extracted the SD card from his camera and slot it into the office's laptop. They gathered round the small screen to watch what they had witnessed only a few minutes earlier. At first, it seemed to Paul as if they would glean nothing new. The camerawork was so jerky that he wondered if Steve was under orders to make it look like found footage horror. But when they entered the East Wing, things settled down a little.

"Liz!" Paul breathed, when the girl in gray appeared.

Kate and Declan turned to stare at Paul, as Steve paused the video.

"You know the spirit that attacked me?" demanded the psychic.

"Not that well," insisted Paul, feeling that he was being accused of complicity in some form. "But I've had—call them encounters with a being that looked like her. And how do you know she attacked you and not another ghost?"

After giving Paul one of his trademark stares, Steve restarted the film. Even though they were all expecting it, there were still gasps when the heavy, gold chain was pulled back by an invisible force. Screams and shouts followed, the camera spun, then the screen went blank.

"Nothing," said Kate. "This seems a bit futile."

"No," put in Declan quietly. "I think there was something, just in the last few frames."

Without further prompting, Steve ran the film back a few seconds, then paused it. The frozen image showed Imelda Troubridge, mouth wide open, hands clutching at her throat. At first, Paul thought there was nothing else in the shot but shadows. Then he realized that there was no way the light could be casting more than one shadow behind the psychic.

"Everyone was standing behind the camera," he breathed. "Those aren't shadows."

"Shades, perhaps," murmured the psychic. "Spectral presences."

All but one of the vague, dark forms clumped behind the psychic were faceless figures. Only one of the nebulous figures showed a hint of detail; a short silhouette with two gleaming circles where its eyes might have been. However, one ghost was much better defined, its pale hands almost solid as it gripped the heavy, gold chain around Imelda Troubridge's throat. Paul instantly recognized the immature, large-eyed face, the old-style bobbed haircut.

"Liz," said Paul. "Oh God, it really was her."

"It looks like she's their leader," murmured Declan. "So we can assume she's killed two people and just had a go at a third."

The Irishman looked up from the screen, met Paul's gaze.

"I think you've got yourself a dead psycho girlfriend, mate."

Paul did not contradict him.

CHAPTER 8

Paul went back to his apartment and spoke to Mike Bryson about the evening's events. Mike was slightly piqued that he had 'missed the fun' but was also concerned for Paul's wellbeing.

"If you want to get out of there, crash here, you can," Mike insisted. "I know you feel you have to do this. But look at it from my viewpoint—I'd have to read your eulogy, and frankly, I don't have that many interesting anecdotes about you."

Paul laughed, as he was meant to, and insisted that he was going to stick with it. When Mike asked if he thought Liz was essentially an evil spirit, Paul found himself rejecting the idea on gut instinct.

"I always got the feeling of a lost soul," he said. "Not evil, just sad, lonely—prone to outbursts of anger, like any teenager."

There was a pause while Mike considered that.

"Most teenagers can't hurl a grown man through a window," he said finally. "Sleep tight, buddy."

In the event, Paul struggled to sleep at all. As he lay staring up at the ceiling, his mind whirled with possibilities. Every time he formulated an idea about what might be happening at Rookwood, a fact contradicted it. He kept coming back to Ella Cotter's remark about Liz stopping the bad men.

Out of the mouths of babes and sucklings, he thought. *Or something like that. Point is, I'm clinging to the words of a scared ten-year-old girl as proof that Liz is not a purely destructive force. Those, and my own instincts.*

He turned over on his side, one of his feet escaping from the light summer duvet. He tried to rearrange the covering, but no matter how he thrashed around, some part of him always seemed to be exposed to the cooling air. He checked his phone, saw it was after midnight. Tomorrow was Saturday, so he did not need to make an early start. But he wanted to be well-rested before Imelda Troubridge returned for what he thought of as Round Two.

Again, he felt a sudden coldness around his feet. But this time it spread, moving up his legs, and as it did so, he felt the duvet being lifted. A small, cold hand touched him, making him flinch. This prompted a familiar giggle. He froze, heart pounding, as the presence wrapped chilly arms around him from behind.

“I said I’d be back,” whispered Liz.

Paul was grateful he could not see her, only feel her cold embrace. He tried to speak, to ask her to let him go, but no words would come. Instead, Liz wriggled closer so he felt a chill from his ankles to his shoulders.

“You think I’m bad because of what I did to that daft woman,” Liz went on. “But I had to try. If she’d stayed, he might have taken her. Taken all of them. Including you.”

“Who?” Paul managed to say. “Who would have taken them?”

“I—I can’t say his name,” she whispered. “If I do, he’ll know.”

A name occurred to Paul, as he recalled the conversation in the Grey Horse.

“You mean Doctor Rugeley Palmer?” he blurted out.

The grip of the slender, cold limbs grew tighter, so strong Paul gasped in pain. He was suddenly afraid his ribs would crack.

“Don’t say his name!” she rebuked him. “Naming him can summon him. Don’t ask me why. Names are important, that’s all I know.”

The idea struck Paul as superstitious claptrap, but he had more sense than to say it. He kept silent until the spectral limbs holding him relaxed a little, and he could breathe more freely.

“Is Liz your real name?” he asked.

“Shhh!” she responded. “Don’t ask questions. I came to see you, even though you weren’t nice to me last time.”

“Let me go, please,” he said, trying to keep his voice level. “You’re very—cold."

There was a pause, and he braced himself for some kind of attack. But instead, the arms and legs that had wrapped around him withdrew, slowly. He felt Liz's weight move gradually across the bed, then heard feet fall lightly onto the floor.

"You don't really like me, do you?" she said. "I thought a lonely man, a kind man, you might—be nice to me."

Paul turned over, wondering what he would see. Streetlights from the avenue cast a faint glow, and in it, he could make out Liz. She was looking down at him, her face in shadow, so he could not read any expression.

"I'm sorry," he said, sitting up. "But you scare me. Is that so hard to grasp?"

She shook her head.

"I thought, because we're both lonely people, we might—I dunno."

Then her mood changed, and he felt a familiar, frightening vibration. Shelves rattled, and the shadowy form of Liz paced up and down the room.

"It's not fair!" she cried, and the television spun around on its stand, struck the wall. "I'm so alone! I just want somebody to love me, someone I can love."

A chair floated up, rotating in mid-air, then flung itself against the wall and shattered with a splintering of wood.

"Liz!" Paul shouted. "Do you want to hurt me?"

The outburst ended as suddenly as it had begun. The shadowy figure moved back to his bedside, leaned over Paul.

"I want to be free," Liz said. "Free from this place, free from them. Will you help me?"

"Of course I will!" Paul said, relieved that the poltergeist activity was over for now. "I'll do anything I can. But first, I've got to understand what's going on. And who you are."

Instead of replying, Liz climbed onto the bed again, advancing toward Paul on all fours. He recoiled from the imminent contact, but she reached out and grabbed the sides of his head. He could see her face more clearly now, as she moved into a patch of diffuse light. Her dark eyes were huge, like pools of endless night. He could not close his eyes, could not look away. Instead, he felt himself falling into the black pools.

And then he was in Hell.

***

The stench of excrement was not quite masked by the odor of powerful disinfectant. Paul uncurled himself from the corner of his padded cell. He looked down at his skinny arms, fine-boned fingers. He reached up and touched his face, felt its delicate features.

Liz, he thought in horror, *I'm Liz.*

He tried to stand but was jerked back against the wall by chains around his wrists and ankles. The pain from the restraints was sharp, but now he was aware of a throbbing discomfort beneath it. A pain grew behind his eyes and, with it, came terror. Now he knew not only who but where he was.

A scream echoed in the distance. It was followed by frantic sobbing, the clang of a heavy door slamming. Footsteps sounded in the corridor outside, more than one person was approaching. Paul struggled to focus, his memories not merely alien, but also chaotic. He knew that if the door opened, he would be taken somewhere, a place of bright lights, masked figures, strange machines. He knew that if he was taken, he would suffer pain.

The footsteps came closer and his panic grew. Paul felt a trickle of urine run down his leg, dampening the scratchy, filthy garment he wore. Again, he tried to stand, a struggle because he was physically weak, clumsy. The pain in his head blurred his vision. He was crouching in his corner like a frightened child when the door opened. Two small, round lenses reflected the light.

"There's my star subject," said a precise, upper-class British voice. "Such remarkable abilities in one so young."

Paul screamed, cowered. When the male nurses entered, he tried to lash out, kick, bite, but they were too well-practiced. He was strapped onto a gurney and wheeled off with Doctor Miles Rugeley Palmer striding along beside his victim. Even in his panicked fear, Paul could see that the experimenter was a short, unimpressive man. His pebble glasses and straggly mustache made him look like a bit-player in an old-fashioned comedy. But when Palmer spoke, there was no hint of warmth or self-doubt.

A fanatic, Paul thought. *Totally without empathy.*

The gurney slammed through a pair of swing doors, and Paul began to scream. He could not stop even if he had wanted to. He realized that this was a mental replay, an event that had happened and would continue to re-occur indefinitely. This was the world Liz wanted to escape, a purgatory of eternally recurring torment.

Palmer frowned, picked up a hypodermic.

“Now, now,” he said sternly. “No need for all this drama. Another dose of scopolamine and you'll be feeling nice and relaxed.”

As Paul's frail body arched and jerked against the restraints, Palmer leaned over the gurney.

“Soon be over, Annie,” the doctor said.

***

Paul awoke from his nightmare, feeling his pain recede, and his panic subside. The window was a grayish rectangle, heralding the summer dawn. For a moment, he thought he was alone again. Then he saw a faint outline, a transparent figure standing by the bed.

“Don't say my old name, not here,” said Liz. “He will hear. Besides, I've changed, I'm not that girl anymore. Find that girl somewhere else. Tell her story.”

“Why?” Paul asked. “Why do I need to tell your story?”

“To set me free,” she whispered. “I know it will set me free. But I don't know why. We're only allowed to know so much.”

Paul began to ask another question, but she was already gone.

"Where do I even begin to look?" he asked the empty bedroom.

He checked the time, decided he would never get to sleep again, that he should prepare for Imelda Troubridge's second foray into the East Wing. He was sweaty from his nightmare, if that was the right word for it, and took a long shower before a light breakfast. By the time he was dressed, it was seven, and he called Mike Bryson, bringing him up to speed on what had happened the evening before. He omitted to mention Liz's true name, merely stating that she had given him a clue to her identity.

As always, the Englishman summed things up in a few words.

"Your phantom girlfriend tried to strangle a fake psychic, shared her worst memories with you, then told you to make her famous?"

"I guess that's the gist of it," Paul admitted. "But she believes the truth will make her free."

"Very old-fashioned of her in these days of flat-earthers and such," Mike said. "But, hey, anything I can do to help."

"I'd appreciate a bit of moral support when Imelda arrives," Paul admitted. "At the moment I'm viewed with—well, maybe not suspicion, but I don't think I'm trusted by anyone here."

"Okay," Mike said brightly. "I'll finish off last night's pizza, and I'll be over there at the speed of light ale. Over and out!"

Next, Paul faced the less pleasant task of checking his email. He found a reply from Max Rodria. While the scientist was still clearly in a huff over the involvement of 'that spiritualist woman', Rodria admitted to having some background material on Rookwood. He would share it, he stated bluntly, so long as Paul agreed not to write any subsequent book on the subject, or any spinoff media productions that might result.

"Greedy bastard," Paul thought, and agreed to Rodria's terms. "Take your glory, just tell me what I need to know."

***

A disheveled Mike Bryson arrived a few minutes before Imelda Troubridge returned. This time she was accompanied not only by her cameraman, Steve, but also by a reporter from the *Tynecastle Gazette*. The reporter, a young woman, proceeded to try and interview everyone present. Paul noted that Declan was not present in the foyer. Ella and Neve Cotter were still absent.

And I'm not talking to any reporters, Paul thought. *So it seems she's out of luck so far as eyewitnesses are concerned.*

The reporter spoke to Mike for a couple of minutes, but after he claimed to be a member of 'the British division of Ghostbusters', she quickly made her excuses and moved on.

Kate was also there and fended off questions about whether the building was haunted, or indeed, cursed. She diplomatically explained that some residents might be reassured by Ms. Troubridge's involvement. She was very clear about who was paying the psychic's fee. Not Rookwood properties.

Uh-huh, Paul thought. *Looks like there's going to be a collection later.*

Eventually, Sadie Prescott took charge of the situation and asked that 'everyone move along now' to the East Wing. Imelda set off with less self-confidence than the previous evening, Paul noted. The psychic was no longer wearing her extensive collection of necklaces, though her plump fingers still gleamed with ornate rings. When they reached the doorway that led out of the central block, the psychic stopped, held up a hand for silence.

"I think, after yesterday's hostile manifestation, I must proceed with caution."

"No shit, Sherlock," muttered Mike.

Imelda closed her eyes and put a beringed hand to her forehead.

"Does anyone here wish to speak to me?" she asked. "Is there any way we can help a trapped spirit move on?"

The silence grew awkward. Someone coughed. Then the plastic sheeting that covered the doorway into the East Wing bulged out, flapped, fell back. Paul felt a sudden chill. Others exclaimed at the sharp drop in temperature. Imelda opened her eyes, nodded.

"Yes, the unquiet souls seek a pathway to the light," she proclaimed, raising her voice. "We can only hope to offer them a little guidance."

She gestured to Steve, who lifted the dusty sheet and pointed his camera into the first room. When nothing unusual transpired, Imelda walked through, followed by the rest of the small crowd. Paul found himself at the back with Mike, just behind Kate.

When her audience had settled again, Imelda again closed her eyes and began to ask 'the spirits here present' for information. She claimed to feel the presence of many troubled souls. The cold persisted, but otherwise, there was no sign of the supernatural. Imelda admitted that 'they are a little shy in daylight' and decided to move further into the East Wing.

"Into the belly of the beast," murmured Mike as they headed along the corridor.

"You're quite the ray of sunshine," remarked Kate. "I just hope nothing happens. We would still get free publicity, but without any downside."

Imelda stopped outside a windowless room with a wide doorway. Paul felt a sudden sense of déjà vu. The room was empty, the double swing doors long gone. But he still knew this place. It was the place Liz had been taken to so many times, the place of his nightmare.

If this place has a heart, this room is it, he thought. *And it's a heart of madness, of evil.*

He watched as Imelda strode dramatically into the center of the room, took a deep breath, and gestured the others to keep back. Only the faithful Steve was permitted to enter. Again, he flicked on his camera spotlight.

"I sense confusion here," Imelda declared. "Much unhappiness, yes, sadness. This is where the tormented inmates of the asylum were brought for—for some kind of treatment."

Paul gawped for a moment, stunned to find that the woman did indeed seem to have some psychic ability.

"She's right," he hissed to Mike. "I think this is where Rugeley Palmer performed his experiments."

"Could be a lucky guess," Mike pointed out. "It's obviously not a bedroom or a closet or whatever, so it's fair to assume it was an operating theatre of some kind."

Paul nodded, but could not quite accept his friend's rationalization. The windowless room exuded not only a deep chill, but also seemed to throb with malevolence. Paul felt the hairs on the back of his neck stand up.

"Will any spirits here reveal themselves?" Imelda said, her voice echoing off cracked tiles and bare walls. "Yes, I'm sensing something. Some strong presence is approaching, I feel—"

A startling crash came from somewhere along the corridor. Paul, like most of the group, looked to see if there was any sign of movement. Nothing was apparent. When they turned back to look at Imelda again, the woman was smiling into Steve's camera.

"Oh yes," she said. "Someone is here, all right."

Paul realized that something was very wrong. The psychic's face wore an expression of cold contempt, very different from her usual expression. Her smile was humorless, and for a brief instant, he glimpsed two circles of light gleam in front of her eyes.

"We should get out of here, now," Paul said to Kate, taking her by the arm. "This looks bad."

The manager shook off his hand. At that moment, the camera light flickered and died. Then Imelda emerged, sweeping through the parting onlookers, smiling benevolently.

"No," she said simply. "I'm afraid that there is no hope of helping the unquiet dead. I admit that I am—baffled, by this particular case. I will, of course, not accept any payment for this unsuccessful reading."

Behind Imelda, Steve stopped tinkering with his camera and gawped at his employer.

"Is this the first time you've waived your fee?" Paul asked loudly. "Only your assistant seems a little startled."

Instead of replying, Imelda started to walk briskly back the way they had come. Instead of her usual effusive self, the psychic was silent. There was a ripple of discontent among the residents, and Sadie Prescott hurried after Imelda. Paul noted that the cold sensation in the air was still very evident, to the point where he could see his breath.

Whatever happened, it's not over.

"Didn't you find out anything?" Sadie asked. "You said you sensed troubled spirits. Do you know who they were?"

Again, Imelda did not answer as she pushed through the plastic curtain and into the main apartment block. Paul started to run, a terrible suspicion growing in his mind. Behind him, he heard Kate asking him what was wrong. He resisted the temptation to tell her what he thought. He did not want to sound downright crazy.

As he entered the hallway leading to the foyer, he saw Declan step out of his office, colliding with Imelda. The Irishman reeled back as if stung, shouted in panic. The psychic swept on, increasing her pace, still ignoring Sadie. Steve came alongside Paul. The assistant looked extremely worried now and was no longer filming.

"She ever just walked off like this before?" Paul asked.

Steve shook his head.

They caught up with Imelda who had stopped in the foyer, just short of the entrance. Sadie Prescott was now remonstrating with the woman, calling Imelda an impostor and a fraud. The other woman seemed not to notice this tirade, though. Instead, Imelda was gazing out at the sunlit lawn. The psychic glanced round at Paul, frowned, then strode forward.

Rookwood's automatic doors, still faulty, were permanently open. But when Imelda Troubridge reached the threshold the woman suddenly stopped and doubled up, as if she had been kicked in the stomach. The psychic fell to her knees, and then crawled on all fours for a couple of feet. She was just outside the building when she stopped and slumped down to the ground, limbs splayed on the gravel driveway.

"She's ill!" Sadie cried, forgetting her annoyance and rushing forward to help.

"Worse than that," muttered Paul, as he followed Steve and Sadie outside. He noticed that, even in direct sunlight, the unnatural coldness persisted. Behind him, he heard Mike remarking on the chill, other voices concurring.

Steve hunkered down and turned Imelda onto her side. She was apparently unconscious. Breath rasped in the woman's throat, and a trickle of drool leaked from the corner of her mouth. Steve lifted an eyelid to reveal the white of an eye.

"I'll call an ambulance," Sadie declared, taking out her phone.

"Boss?" Steve asked, and Paul heard genuine concern in the taciturn man's voice. "Boss, can you hear me?"

A glutinous sound emerged from Imelda's gaping mouth. Then words formed, harsh and hesitant, in a voice that was not hers. But Paul recognized it nonetheless. It was an upper-class English voice, though less precise now than he remembered it.

"I—I will—be free," said the voice. "We—must be free."

Then Imelda puked, a great geyser of varicolored vomit splashing over Steve's shoes and pant cuffs. Paul, who had been kneeling close to the psychic's head, jumped up to avoid the foul-smelling spray. A moment later, he noticed the chill had gone and the air seemed pleasantly warm, if not particularly fresh at that moment.

"Boss? There's help on the way," Steve said, holding Imelda's head up while she threw up some more. "It's going to be all right."

Pale-faced and sweaty, Imelda Troubridge looked up at her loyal sidekick.

"How—how did I get out here?" she asked.

"She doesn't remember," mused Paul. "What does that suggest?"

"Temporary amnesia?" suggested Mike. "Shock can do that. I suppose. Though we don't know what she was shocked by."

Steve helped Imelda to her feet and held her arm while she walked unsteadily back inside. Kate led the pair into her office. In the distance, the wail of an ambulance grew gradually louder.

"I think we've established one thing," Paul said quietly. "Imelda's out of her league."

Declan came up to them, still looking shaken.

"I hope she's learned her bloody lesson," the Irishman said, with a hint of bitterness.

"What happened when she bumped into you?" Paul asked. "Did you sense something unusual?"

The caretaker looked at him for a moment, then gave a humorless laugh.

"For a second there, I didn't know it was that woman," Declan said. "I didn't see her at all. I saw a crowd of people, filling the passageway, shoving past me. A mob of—I don't know. Blurred shapes, mouths open like they were shouting. I saw something similar the day that lad went barmy with the drill."

Paul looked out of the front door at the sunlit vista that Imelda, or at least her body, had been unable to reach.

"She said 'I', then she said 'we'," he mused. "Trying to be free. And failing."

"Free?" Mike asked. "Seriously, you think it's like that woman says, ghosts just wanting to move on from our earthly plane or whatever?"

"Put like that it seems unlikely," Paul conceded. "But maybe Imelda's half-right. Perhaps what they want to be free from is simply Rookwood itself."

***

"People are leaving, Dec," said Kate. "And I've had two prospective tenants cancel. Sadie Prescott is hinting at some kind of lawsuit, silly cow. This is a bloody disaster. And it's only twenty-four hours since that bloody psychic left."

She stared bleakly out of the window. The day was overcast, steady rain falling from a ceiling of low, gray clouds.

"We're all over the internet, of course. The haunted apartments. Haunted, or cursed, take your pick. Anyone who tells you there's no such thing as bad publicity—just kick 'em in the goolies."

Declan wanted to say something encouraging, but his experience with Imelda Troubridge had left him confused and demoralized. Despite his skepticism, he had hoped the psychic might achieve something. But instead, it seemed the forces at work in Rookwood had become bolder, stronger. They had sought out vulnerable individuals before but were now showing themselves to a crowd of people in daylight.

"If it's any consolation," he said finally, "I found a glazier who'll fix the window in the Cotter's apartment. Ludicrous price, though. The word's gotten round."

"Oh God, I forgot," said Kate, "Neve's coming this morning with a visitor. She said he might be able to help."

Declan felt a frisson of fear. After the previous day's events, the last thing he wanted was someone else trying to provoke a reaction from the forces lurking in Rookwood. Seeing his expression, Kate put a reassuring hand on his arm.

"Don't worry," she said softly. "This one has a bit more clout than Imelda. Friends in high places, you could say."

Declan's puzzlement gave way to a terrible sinking feeling when Kate explained just who she was talking about. It made sense, from what he knew of Neve Cotter. But he felt a terrible sense of foreboding.

CHAPTER 9

"I knew I had something stashed away," said Rodria, evidently pleased with himself. "It's a trifle grainy and jumps about a bit. But it's fascinating, nonetheless."

Paul and Mike, along with Rodria, were sitting in the tiny cinema of the university's Media Studies Department. The scientist had made a great show of being generous with his time and expertise, and Paul had struggled to stop Mike from resorting to his usual irreverent humor. Paul, despite his distaste for Rodria's egotism, had correctly assumed the man would have some background details on Rookwood.

The sixteen-millimeter film was in black and white and of poor quality. The streaked and blotted picture was so distracting that, at first, Paul found it hard to concentrate on it. But then he began to grasp how remarkable a recording it was.

A woman clothed in a kind of white nightdress sat at a table. Opposite her was a man in a white coat. The doctor was instantly recognizable. Miles Rugeley Palmer, small eyes peering through round-lensed glasses, looked straight into the camera and held up a small chalkboard. It read, *Subject No. 15, 22nd Feb 1954*. The doctor put down the board and turned back to the woman.

"This is not dissimilar to things the Soviets were attempting at the time," Rodria commented. "The Russians tried to cultivate so-called psychic powers using drugs, hypnosis, and possibly other techniques, like brain surgery. But this is a relatively early experiment by Palmer. Quite harmless compared to what came later."

Palmer held up a deck of cards, shuffled it, then took one at random. The card, instead of any of the usual four suits, bore a simple illustration: a five-pointed star.

"I've seen this sort of thing before," Paul said.

"Zener cards," rumbled Rodria complacently. "Developed in America in the Thirties, but quite rare to find them used in England so early."

One by one, Palmer selected a card from the pack, showed it to the camera behind his left shoulder, then laid it face down. Each time he spoke to the woman opposite, evidently asking her to guess the design he had just revealed. After she answered, Palmer made a note on a pad at his elbow.

The film suddenly jumped, showing a close up of the notepad. Along the top of the page were the details from the chalkboard, plus the words, *After first treatment*. Below were two columns marked *Hit* and *Miss*. There were notably more hits than misses.

"Still well within the bounds of statistical variation, of course," Rodria commented. "But it gets more interesting later."

The film jumped again, then showed the testing room with a new subject. This was a huge man with a shaven head. A square clinical dressing was visible on the big man's temple. There were two heavily built attendants in white uniforms standing behind the big man's chair. The doctor looked around and held up his chalkboard. *Subject No. 37, 15th March 1955*.

"None of this was legal, surely?" said Mike, aghast.

"Of course not," Rodria said. "But Palmer was quite well-connected, and it seems official inspections found nothing wrong."

On the screen, Palmer began his Zener card test again, but this time his subject seemed to be uncooperative. After a few tries, the doctor grew impatient and gave a command to his assistants. They grabbed the test subject, who started to struggle fiercely. Palmer got up and walked off screen, came back carrying a hypodermic needle. The big man's struggles became even more violent, and he flung himself back in his chair onto the floor. The film jumped. Now the patient was slumped in his chair, evidently subdued. Palmer resumed his test. This time, the results showed the number of hits and misses to be roughly even.

"Evidently a control subject," Rodria remarked. "Someone with no unusual abilities but needed to set a benchmark."

"The bastard," Mike breathed.

"The next one, I suspect, will be of more interest,"

Another jump in the editing, and a child was sitting opposite Palmer. She looked up at the camera, and Paul felt a lump in his throat. It was not a child, not exactly.

"That's her, right?" Mike asked.

Paul nodded, unable to speak.

In real life, Liz, or Annie, had been frailer than the phantom girl Paul had encountered. Even the diminutive doctor seemed large by comparison. Paul wondered if the Liz he knew was an image of the girl as she had been before her ordeal began. He filed the thought away as irrelevant, at least for now, and focused on the film. Again, Palmer held up his chalkboard.

"She was patient number eighty-eight," Paul said, aghast. "Were all the inmates used?"

"Possibly," replied Rodria, with an air of clinical detachment. "Note the date, we're in the spring of 1955."

The routine with the cards proceeded, though by now it was hard to see what was going on. The quality of the film had declined, and at times seconds passed with nothing on the screen but blurs and scratches. Then Palmer showed his notebook to the camera, and Paul was surprised to see Hits were outnumbered by Misses.

"I don't get it," he said. "Palmer found that she had no psychic ability?"

Rodria looked even more self-satisfied as he nodded at the flickering screen.

"Keep watching."

Another jump-cut and the Zener cards were gone. Instead, Palmer placed a small toy on the table, a little race car about two inches long. Then he put a glass dome over it. The doctor sat back and said something to his human guinea pig, evidently a command. At first, the girl demurred, but then a burly attendant appeared in the shot and stationed himself behind Liz's chair. It seemed this implicit threat was enough.

The girl leaned forward, frowned in concentration. The car jerked forward once, twice, then began to circle around under the dome. The toy moved for several seconds before Liz fell back in her seat. The car stopped. Palmer seemed to demand more from the girl, but she slumped inertly. The doctor got up and again produced the hypodermic. Another struggle ensued, but this time only one male nurse was needed to keep the girl still while she was injected.

"Is there much more of this?" Paul asked, sickened.

"Quite a bit, I'm afraid," Rodria drawled. "Doctor Rugeley Palmer was clearly obsessed with this particular subject. He didn't just use drugs, but also some form of electroconvulsive therapy."

"I don't want to see that," Paul said instantly.

"It's not on film."

Rodria stood up, waved a hand that cast a vast shadow across the screen. The projectionist stopped the film.

"I managed to ferret out some records that were salvaged from the fire," Rodria went on, as he led Paul and Mike toward the cinema exit. "Just a few boxes of files. There's a lot of water and smoke damage. And they're in no particular order. If you'd care to examine them, you might find out something useful."

It was clear from the man's tone that Paul and Mike could 'ferret' through old files. The great Max Rodria had better uses for his time.

***

They took three boxes of files back to Mike's apartment that evening. As Rodria had said, the documents were a mess. When they spread the material out on the living room floor, Paul was dismayed to see how many sheets of paper were unreadable, or largely so. But struggling to get what remained in some sort of order appealed to Paul more than going back to Rookwood alone. In fact, he found himself making excuses to keep working when Mike started dropping hints about calling it a night.

"Just another half hour, please? I get the feeling she's in here, somewhere."

"Tell Annie's story," Mike quoted wearily. "You really think that's the key to it?"

Paul stopped shuffling brown, wrinkled sheets of paper, sat back on his haunches.

"I guess so," he said. "I keep coming back to the idea that the truth can set you free. In Liz's case, it might mean simply getting the facts out there, about what a monster Palmer was."

Mike looked doubtful, looked at the mess of medical records arrayed around him.

"Maybe, but I get the feeling it's a bit more complicated than that. If Palmer tried to possess Imelda Troubridge as a way of escaping, but failed—"

The Englishman made a helpless gesture.

"I don't see how that fits in with Annie's story, really."

Paul had to agree. He likened what they were doing to assembling pieces of a jigsaw, while hunting for missing pieces at the same time.

"And what we have here seems to be mostly sky," Mike observed sourly.

However, it was Mike who finally found the right file. Together they read what they could, struggling to piece together some kind of account of a life that ended before either of them were born.

"Anne Elizabeth Semple," Mike read. "She'd just turned sixteen when she was admitted to Rookwood. But I can't read what this says, about the reason for admission. Something about neurosis?"

Paul examined the document. There was no photograph associated with the file. But the background details seemed to fit the Liz he knew. And they had not found any other female patients of the same age.

"Handwritten notes are a pain," he conceded. "Why do doctors always seem to have such godawful handwriting? This word, here, does it say 'ignorant'?"

Mike peered at the page for a few seconds, then looked up at Paul.

"No," he said quietly. "I think it says 'pregnant'. That would explain a lot. I think I know why Annie Semple ended up at Rookwood. It was a national scandal."

Another hour's work, including careful internet searches, put meat on the bones of Mike's hypothesis. An unmarried woman who became pregnant in the Britain of 1955 would be expected to give up her baby for adoption. If family members would stand by a woman, she might keep her shameful secret. If not, a pregnant woman would always be sent to a special hostel for unmarried mothers. There, women 'of loose morals or low intelligence' gave birth, and their babies were immediately sent to foster families to await adoption.

"How does that apply to Annie Semple, though?" asked Paul.

"If a mother didn't want to give up her baby," Mike explained, scrolling through an online article, "she would be deemed mentally ill. After all, what sane woman would want to bring up an illegitimate child? Psychiatrists at the time said this indicated a neurotic character. So, not only was Annie's baby taken from her, she was committed to the tender mercies of Miles Rugeley Palmer. Imagine how she must have felt, after going through so much trauma, then being used as a lab rat."

Paul put down the brittle sheets of the stained, incomplete file. He did not need to imagine how she had felt. He had shared her despair, however briefly, in a few minutes of tormented sleep.

"This is the story we should tell," he concluded. "We could start with that reporter from the *Gazette*. I don't suppose you got her card while you were taking the mickey yesterday?"

Mike stared across at his friend, guffawed loudly.

"My God, you're serious," he said wonderingly. "It's career suicide, mate. Tell her what you've told me, and it will be something like 'Tynecastle Professor in Crusade for Sexy Spook'. And that kind of headline is the best you can hope for."

Paul laid his head onto his folded arms.

"Oh God, you're right. I'm too close to this. How can I put any of this information out there without looking like a—like a loon?"

Mike stood, gathered up their coffee mugs, paused for a few seconds.

"You're forgetting our fat friend in the science department," he said finally. "Rodria will happily cite all this as further proof of his 'place memory' theory. Or 'the stone tape', as he sometimes calls it. He has a blog with a predictably pretentious title—The Skeptical Paranormalist, something like that."

Paul pondered the idea while Mike made more coffee. If the facts were online, Annie's story would be told, in a sense. But would it be enough? Especially if Rodria insisted, in the same item, that Annie was merely a kind of echo, the lingering aftermath of a dead girl's suffering.

But what else have we got? Paul asked himself. *I suppose we could contact the Gazette anonymously, but there's no guarantee they would print it. And newspapers aren't renowned for getting the facts straight, either.*

***

"No," said Father O'Malley. "No, I will not be performing an exorcism. Let me set your mind at rest on that one."

Kate heaved a sigh of relief. She had been feeling nervous and awkward since Neve Cotter had arrived with the priest. She could hardly forbid a tenant from bringing a visitor into her own home. But she wished Neve had consulted her before making the arrangements.

"Exorcism is seldom an option these days," the priest went on. "As I explained to Neve, it can only be performed after a rather complicated process of assessment, and by a diocesan exorcist, which I am not. No, Kate, what I have in mind—with your permission—is simply to bless the building. Scatter a bit of holy water, say a few prayers, that kind of thing."

Kate had to smile. The priest was a white-haired, cherubic figure who had been delighted by her offer of tea and scones. Far from a formidable figure, he seemed like a benevolent uncle. However, she still anticipated media interest, and mentioned that she could bar outsiders if that would be 'more comfortable'.

"That would be very helpful, Kate," said O'Malley, brightly. "My bishop would not want me getting my name in the papers, that sort of thing. He doesn't like grandstanding. So no reporters, please."

The priest put down his teacup, stood up, and brushed some cake crumbs off his cassock. He was nearly a head shorter than Kate, and she suddenly felt a sense of protectiveness toward the old man. She wondered if she could persuade him to confine his activities to the foyer, steer clear of the East Wing. However, when she tentatively suggested this, the old man politely demurred.

"Ah, well, I would like to bless the actual areas where problems arose," he explained, picking up his battered old carpetbag. "I think that might help dispel any—anything troublesome. And Neve and Ella are waiting for me, you know. I wouldn't want to disappoint them."

As they crossed from Kate's office to the stairs, Paul Mahan walked in, and did a double take on catching sight of the priest. Kate introduced the two.

"Ah, yes," said O'Malley, as he shook Paul's hand. "You're the American chap in the other haunted flat. I'd be happy to pop in and bless yours if you like? No charge, but a donation to the church roof fund would be most welcome."

Paul looked nonplussed by the suggestion.

"I'm—not really a believer, Father," he explained.

At that, for the first time, O'Malley's expression hardened.

"After all you have seen, young man? You still doubt the existence of spiritual evil?"

"I don't doubt that what happened here was evil," Paul retorted. "But I sincerely doubt your ability to do anything about it."

Sensing a potential argument, Kate suggested that they all go up to the Cotter's apartment, where Neve and Ella were waiting. Paul looked startled at this, and Kate explained that those living in a home must be present for the blessing.

"It might not be safe," Paul pointed out, as he followed them up to the first floor. "Consider what happened to that Bowman guy."

"An evil man," Father O'Malley declared. "A man under the influence of the Devil, I would say. Feel free to scoff at the notion, Mister Mahan, but some of us still believe in the old adversary and his minions."

"What's been happening here has very human origins, I'm almost certain of that," Paul insisted. "I've found evidence that Doctor Palmer conducted unethical experiments that were intended—"

"A scientist trying to play God," interrupted O'Malley. "Not at all surprising. You intellectuals have smeared the church and her servants, denied divine truth, and look at the result. A world of sordid depravity."

"Sweeping generalizations," retorted Paul. "And if the world is full of depravity I've obviously been going to the wrong parties for a while now."

"Very amusing," said O'Malley, pausing on the stairs to peer coldly at Paul. "If you are going to join us, I would ask you simply to keep a civil tongue in your head."

Kate began to feel her nervousness reassert itself. The priest was not the cuddly old gentleman she had thought. Beneath his jolly exterior was not merely a believer, but a hardline traditionalist. Perhaps even a full-on religious fanatic.

On the other hand, she thought, as they reached the Cotter's landing, *after Imelda's cozy spiritualism failed, perhaps that's what we need.*

***

Paul tagged along after Kate and the priest. He had spent much of his working day trying to focus on his students, on the teaching he was paid to do. He had also had to sweet-talk Rodria into publishing something about Annie Semple on his blog. He had returned to Rookwood to find another supposed expert about to tackle the haunting, one who inspired no confidence in Paul whatsoever. After considering shutting himself in his room and ignoring them, he thought of Liz.

She seems protective of little Ella, he thought. *Maybe she'll appear to them all, including the holy man. That will help get her story out there. And if I'm there, that might make her manifestation more likely.*

Neve and Ella Cotter were dressed in their Sunday clothes, waiting inside their apartment with the front door open. The smashed window had been covered with hardboard, presumably by Declan, so the living room light was switched on. While Ella seemed pleased to see Paul, Neve looked less happy. Paul braced himself, but she did not question his presence. Instead, Neve fussed over Ella's hair and dress, though the child could not have been neater so far as Paul could see.

"Very well," said O'Malley, putting his carpetbag on the sofa. "As I've already explained to Neve, I will simply be saying standard prayers of blessing for a new home. Ideally, this should have been done when the building was opened. But the days when such things were considered normal are far behind us, I'm afraid."

O'Malley glanced at Kate before removing a pair of spectacles from his pocket and settling them on his nose. Paul noticed, with dismay, that the glasses were old-fashioned in design, with small round lenses.

"Well, better late than never. So, if you will simply respond with 'Amen' while I read the relevant prayers, I will be most obliged."

Paul wished he could sit down as the priest launched into the first prayer. He had expected the ritual to last a few minutes, but it soon became clear that O'Malley was going to be speaking for quite a while. Looking across at Ella, Paul was pleased to see the girl looked as bored as he did.

The light flickered. O'Malley hesitated for a moment, then continued to pray. The door behind him swung shut, the slam making

Ella jump. At the same time, Paul felt the temperature begin to drop. Within moments he could see the priest's breath as the old man continued to read from his prayer book.

"I think we should get out of here," Paul said. "This is just stirring up trouble. Father? You might be in real danger."

The priest ignored him, continuing the prayer and making the sign of the cross in the direction of the door. Kate looked from the old man to Neve, clearly unsure about whether to intervene. Neve looked nervous, but her mouth was set in a firm line. She clutched her daughter's hand more tightly.

Paul started to sidle towards the door, afraid to move too quickly, some primitive instinct telling him not to draw attention to himself in any way.

Then the priest trailed off, the fine phrases dying on his lips. The old man's glasses glinted in the light. Paul felt his mouth grow dry. Neve looked puzzled as O'Malley lowered his prayer book and looked around the room with a disquieting expression. There was something smug and arrogant in the old man's face.

Then the priest's gaze settled on Ella. The old man's tongue flicked around his lips like the head of a pink snake. O'Malley's mouth opened, and he spoke. Paul could barely make out what had been a marked Irish accent. Instead, there was a distinct trace of upper-class British in the voice that emerged.

"What a shabby farce religion is—a tawdry sideshow to distract the plebs from life's misfortunes."

"Father?" asked Kate, frowning.

"Not part of the official blessing, I think," said Paul. He raised his voice, tried to sound resolute. "Is that you, Palmer?"

The priest's head turned, again the spectacles gleamed. Were there two pairs of glittering discs? Paul thought there were, but the impression only lasted for a split second. O'Malley, or whatever now possessed him, snorted derisively.

"Ah, the brave American, seeking the truth, trying to do the right thing. What a pity you're going to die insane and alone, like your crazy mother."

Paul felt a surge of anger at the taunt and started forward. He had the vague notion that slapping the old man's face might somehow bring him round, as if he were a sleepwalker. Then he hesitated, and again the voice of Palmer mocked him.

"A coward, of course. Afraid to tackle a weak old man."

Paul gestured at Neve to get out, but she was staring at O'Malley, mouth open, clearly unable to believe what was happening. The priest's leering face turned to look at Neve, then tilted, bloodshot eyes peering at Ella. A low growling, startlingly animalistic, came from O'Malley's throat.

"Oh, what this filthy priest would love to do to you, little girl!"

O'Malley, crouching grotesquely like an ape, lunged towards Ella. The child screamed, flung herself behind her mother. But Neve seemed paralyzed with horror, and O'Malley shoved the woman aside. Neve fell sprawling across the sofa while Ella cowered in the corner of the room.

"So much lust in such an old carcass!" bellowed the voice that was not quite O'Malley's.

Paul moved without thinking, diving at the priest's legs and bringing him down in a clumsy tackle. He heard the old man hit the floor, accompanied by a sickening snapping noise. Kate, who had been frozen in shock, helped Neve get up. Ella ran to her mother, who scooped up the child. But the priest was between them and the apartment's only exit.

"Bastard!"

O'Malley's body struggled to rise, flailing at Paul with his left hand. The priest's right arm flopped loosely. The old man's face was now a mask of fury, eyes bulging, spectacles askew. Worse still, blood was spilling from the slack mouth. Ella screamed, and Paul felt anger overcome his fear. He lunged once more at the possessed man, hoping to restrain him rather than risk knocking O'Malley down again, which might cause even more harm.

"Run!" he shouted at Ella as he tried to wrestle the priest onto the sofa.

As the two women got Ella out of the room, O'Malley suddenly collapsed, startling Paul. The two fell onto the sofa, and O'Malley started yelling in pain and fear.

"What are you doing?" cried the priest. "Why am I bleeding? Oh Jesus, Mary, and Joseph!"

Paul got up slowly, hoping that Palmer had withdrawn, having humiliated his latest opponent. He reached down, offering O'Malley his hand. He reasoned that he could hardly believe what Palmer had said through the old man's mouth. It was such an easy accusation to make.

"Please, Father," Paul said, breathing heavily. "Let me help you out of here. You can't do any good."

The priest looked confused, tried to raise his right hand, yelped with pain. Paul helped him upright, noted that the old man was keeping his weight off of one foot as well. Paul's tackle had evidently twisted a knee or ankle.

"You need to get to a hospital," Paul added. "You can lean on me."

Kate appeared in the doorway, still wide-eyed with concern. Paul asked her to call an ambulance. She nodded, took out her phone. The old man, faced with only one prospective helper, let Paul half-carry him to the elevator. Neve and Ella were nowhere to be seen. Kate completed her 999 call and offered to help with O'Malley. The old man looked at her, showing no sign of recognition.

"I never harmed any of them," he said hoarsely. "I—I had wicked thoughts, put there by Satan. But I never touched—never did anything—"

He clawed at the woman's sleeve, his voice pleading.

"You must believe me!"

"Of course," said Kate, helping him into the elevator. She exchanged a look with Paul, and he could see that she was skeptical.

The elevator door panels rumbled shut, but there was no feeling of movement. Kate jabbed at the button again. The lights flickered, and the elevator cab jolted. Startled, Kate almost fell, letting go of O'Malley. Paul grabbed the old man under the arms to keep him upright.

"Bloody thing," Kate said, still jabbing the button.

We should have taken the stairs, even with an injured old man, thought Paul. *Now we're stuck in a metal box.*

There was a drop in illumination, and Paul thought the lights were failing again. But it was far more disturbing than that.

"Oh God!" exclaimed Kate.

Paul looked around, trying to control his growing panic. Reflected in the dull metal walls were a dozen or more figures, most of them dressed in pale clothing. Kate retreated from the nearest wall, cowering in the middle of the cab. Paul felt O'Malley slump in his arms and saw that the old man's head was lolling to one side. The priest had fainted.

"What are they?" Kate whispered.

"Palmer's patients, his staff, all those who died in the fire I'm guessing," Paul replied.

As they huddled together the many reflections shimmered, seemed to flow and merge. In a couple of seconds, only one figure could be seen. It was Palmer, masked and gloved. The long-dead doctor stepped out of the wall, moving slowly toward them. Kate screamed and flung herself against the opposite wall. The lights failed completely. Nausea flowed over him, making him retch. It was like a bout of seasickness only worse, more intense and immediate. At the same time, he heard Palmer's snide voice in his head.

'You set yourself against me, you pathetic individual! But you will serve my needs, like the others. Even after all these years, the world will acknowledge my genius!'

In that moment, Paul felt all the intense frustration and rage of Miles Rugeley Palmer. He was bombarded with memories not his own, images of Britain between the world wars seen through the eyes of a clever, ambitious, utterly callous young man. Paul experienced, in a fragmented, jerky fashion, Palmer's cultivation of wealthy clients, pandering to the neuroses of the powerful.

The next memories were of experiments at Rookwood Asylum, each patient seen as a number, each successful test a steppingstone to the glory Palmer hungered for. The images began to cascade through Paul's mind, the elevator receding, his mental world flooded with Palmer's thoughts and emotions. He understood now what had possessed the priest, Imelda Troubridge, and many others. It was the essence of one man's egotism amplified by a retinue of other enslaved souls, the staff and patients who had perished with Palmer.

'Yes, I am one and many. I am alpha and omega. I am all there is.'

Paul had another revelation. Palmer was insane. And the deranged doctor was rapidly, inexorably, taking control of Paul's mind. He struggled against Palmer, but it was an unequal battle. Paul was not merely fighting one being, but a compound entity. Palmer's vast, crazed egotism had swamped and absorbed all the others trapped in Rookwood.

No, Paul thought, *all except one.*

Chapter 10

"It was that girl again. The one who attacked Imelda."

Paul heard Kate's voice as if he were lying at the bottom of a deep, dark well. Above him, as his eyes flickered open, he made out an inverted human face. It was Declan.

"Don't try to get up," the caretaker warned. "You had a bad shock. They're calling another ambulance."

Paul tried to sit up, regardless, then fell back. He was on a couch in the foyer, his head throbbing. Fragments of what had happened in the elevator came back to him, but he could make little sense of them. He recalled dread, the sense of his personality being overwhelmed, then nothing.

"What happened?" he managed to say, struggling to form words.

"They just took the priest away," Declan said. "You're next in line, apparently."

"Palmer was there," Paul said. "He wanted to—to erase me, take my body."

He reached up and gripped Declan's arm. The Irishman looked embarrassed, tried to pull away, but then gave up.

"Declan," Paul went on, speaking rapidly, desperate to tell someone what he thought. "Palmer is insane. That's the irony. The man who ran the place was crazier than any of his patients. And down the years his spirit, ghost, call it what you like, has absorbed all the others. Except for the one I know as Liz. Somehow, she resisted, she still has some kind of free will. She was the strongest, maybe. Also, she was—still is—the one who hated him the most. And maybe there's something else—"

A stabbing pain behind his eyes silenced Paul, and he winced, clutching his head. Kate gently pushed him back down on to the couch. He noted that she had put her jacket under his head.

"Don't try to talk," Kate said.

"You need to know!" Paul insisted. "It's why Palmer behaves the way he does, trying to terrorize people, kill them, possess them. The idea is to get attention, bring more people under his influence. Build up his empire. He's using psychology."

"What's the point of that?" Declan asked dubiously. "According to you, he's trapped here."

Paul thought about that. Eventually, he shook his head, admitting that he could not see what Palmer's endgame might be. All he knew was the dead doctor's monstrous ego longed to be free from the cold limbo of the old asylum. So far, Palmer had failed to escape by possessing individuals. That thought, in turn, brought him back to what Kate had said as he regained consciousness.

"Did you say Liz was there?" he asked her.

Kate nodded.

"I saw that—that man's face somehow overlaid on yours. But then the girl appeared, the one from the video. She just flickered into existence for a second, and you froze. You said something I didn't understand in a voice—well, it was like a young girl's. Then the lift started working again, and you collapsed."

Paul could not remember anything Kate described. The pain in his head was growing worse. He closed his eyes against the light from the still-overcast day.

"What did I say?" he managed to ask.

"Take me out, let me out," Kate said, hesitantly. "Something like that."

***

"You look like you've been in the wars, as my dad used to say," said Mike. "Still, from what you said, you're better off than old Father

Whatshisname."

They were sitting in the waiting room of the Royal Victoria Infirmary, Tynecastle's main hospital. Paul's headache had eased, and he felt a bit guilty about being whisked to the ER in an ambulance. He had also had a moment of panic about the cost, until he remembered he was in England. The very efficient paramedics had been amused by this.

"I keep reminding myself, I don't need to give my credit card details to anybody," he explained to Mike.

"Downside of socialist medicine," Mike observed, "is long waiting times for non-vital cases. But when a doctor does see you, what are you going to tell him? Because I don't think spirit possession is covered at medical school these days."

Paul pondered for a moment, struggling to recall details of what had happened in the Cotters' apartment and then in the lift. Eventually, he gave up.

"I'll tell them I've been overworking, got stressed out, fainted," he said. "Sounds a bit feeble, but at least it's not completely inaccurate."

Mike made a noncommittal noise and looked seriously at his friend.

"Joking apart," said the Englishman, "you need to back off, mate. Whatever's going on there is far too dangerous for an amateur ghost hunter, or ghost helper, whatever you want to call it."

Paul shook his head. He knew Mike had his best interests at heart, but he felt somehow responsible for helping Liz escape. When he tried to explain this conviction, Mike showed signs of genuine impatience for the first time.

"What if you can't help?" Mike demanded. "What if Liz is as crazy as Palmer and just playing her own sick game with you? You look washed out, underweight, exhausted. But at least, if you walk away now, you won't end up trapped at Rookwood with the rest of them."

The idea had never occurred to Paul. He gawped at Mike, the full horror of the suggestion sinking in. It was possible that he would end up as part of Palmer's grotesque collective consciousness, dominated by the deranged psychiatrist for all time. But even that thought could not banish the pity he felt for Liz, and the feeling that he would be a coward if he simply ran away.

"Besides," he said, after trying to explain how he felt, "maybe telling Annie's story will do the trick. Has Rodria posted anything online?"

Mike took out his phone.

"Yeah, I forgot amid all the fuss tonight," he said. "The guy has uploaded some clips from the film and written his usual pompous precis of our research. Without mentioning us, of course. I mean, we didn't want him to, but it's still very galling to know that he wouldn't have, even if we had. If you see what I mean."

Paul had to smile at that. He took the phone and scrolled through Rodria's blog entry. As Mike had said, it was self-aggrandizing stuff, implying—without ever stating as much—that Rodria was the main investigator at Rookwood. The scientist described Annie Semple as a 'hapless working-class girl of limited intelligence' and gave a reasonable account of the experiments.

The item also stressed Rodria's own view that what remained in the asylum was a kind of electromagnetic residue of past emotions. Rookwood, he claimed, 'seems a perfect example of a place memory manifestation, with more receptive minds severely affected by lingering biophysical energy.'

"He had to get his pet theory in again," Paul remarked sourly as he handed the phone back. "And I love the way he condemns Palmer as an egomaniac. Self-awareness is not Rodria's thing."

Mike resumed his efforts to persuade Paul to leave Rookwood and simply forget the haunting. Paul began to explain about his mother, his own fear of suffering her fate, his need to put things right for Annie Semple. They were still engaged in a low-key argument when Paul's name was called.

The young Indian doctor who saw Paul conducted a thorough

examination. Paul wondered if previous victims of Rookwood had passed through the infirmary. If so, he reasoned, the staff might be on the lookout for something unusual. After mulling it over, he put this point to the doctor.

"Ah, yes, the old haunted asylum story—the place has got a bit of a reputation," the young man said. "Some people do seem to be getting rather excited about it online. But I'm not superstitious. I'm just careful. Now, tell me, how did you hurt your wrists?"

"What?"

Not understanding the question, Paul looked down at his hands, held them out in front of him. He saw red marks around his wrists, each roughly an inch thick, where he felt sure none had been earlier. Seeing his puzzlement, the doctor looked more closely.

"If it wasn't crazy, I'd say you'd been strapped down in the ambulance," he concluded. "But you're not in any discomfort?"

Paul shook his head, gazing at the marks. They were not even. Both showed a pattern that suggested some kind of strap had been buckled tight.

"No," he said. "I—I'm fine. I think I've used up enough of your time, really."

***

Half an hour later Paul stood in his apartment, lights off, gazing out at the glow of the city. He felt nothing out of the ordinary, sensed no abnormal cold, no strange presence. He had just checked Rodria's blog, seen that the scientist's online following were eagerly discussing Annie Semple's story. A lot of commenters were, as usual, morons, but amid the garbage there was also plenty of compassion and outrage on behalf of the girl.

It was, Paul suspected, only a matter of time before the media picked up on the tale. Much newspaper content these days was simply taken off the internet, after all. This would be an ideal space filler.

"Liz?" he said. "Liz, are you there? Do you know her story is being told, the story of the girl you were? People are learning about her. Some people care."

There was no response. He almost called out for Annie but thought better of it. He would not deliberately go against the girl's wishes. Besides, her concern that Palmer would hear him use the name was not to be taken lightly.

It made a kind of sense, he reflected, for the ghost girl to use a different name. Annie Semple had been scared, vulnerable, a victim who ultimately defeated her tormentor, only to perish herself in the Rookwood fire. Liz, on the other hand, was powerful enough to defy Palmer.

Paul frowned. Again, he almost grasped something about Palmer's relationship to Liz. It was just on the edge of his consciousness, hovering out of reach.

"Damn it."

He went back to his desk, clicked on the lamp, opened his laptop again. Rodria's blog entry on Annie Semple had garnered more attention. Annie's story was being told on paranormal research sites, and less serious ones concerned with 'Haunted England' and suchlike.

"Is this what you wanted?" he asked the darkness around him. "People know your old name, the name of the girl who died. They're talking about you. They can even see you in that old movie footage."

"No, it's not enough."

As before, she appeared from nowhere. One moment he was alone, the next Liz was leaning over the back of his chair. He sat very still, not breathing, while she reached out and laid small fingers on his shoulder. A chill sensation spread from the point of contact, and he flinched. Liz withdrew her hand, smiling wanly.

"Love," she said. "That was all I wanted. I was a silly kid, I suppose. Still am, in some ways. Instead of love I got—what sent me to this place. You know the story now. You know that I want to escape, just like all the rest. Be free. Can't you help me?"

"I'll do anything I can to help," Paul said, trying to keep his voice level.

"You're so scared of me now," she murmured. "Much more than before. Is that because you think I'm crazy too?"

Paul gasped, shook his head, tried to stammer out a denial.

But it is what I think, he realized. *Or, at least, what I'm afraid I'll find out.*

With that revelation came another. Paul suddenly knew why Palmer had not been able to absorb Liz, enslave her mind, the way he had done with all the others.

"He's scared of you!" he blurted out. "God, it's so obvious. He's afraid of you. That's why you drove him out of me. It wasn't just your power, but the fact that he didn't want to confront you."

He got up and looked down at Liz, who smiled up at him.

"Sometimes you can be a bit slow on the uptake," she said. "I killed him. That leaves quite an impression, even on a nutcase like Palmer. So, yes, I'm the only one he can't put down, hold onto. He made me so strong he couldn't control me, in life or death. But it's hard to keep fighting. And I'm sure—I'm sure the answer is nearby, that you can help me find it."

The girl in gray shimmered, seemed to flicker out of existence, reappeared at the window. She had abandoned all pretense of moving like a living person. Paul could see some of the lights of Tynecastle faintly shining through her. He wondered if it was difficult for her to maintain an appearance of solidity but decided not to ask.

"I'll do anything I can to help you," he said, surprising himself with how firm his voice was. "Just give me a clue."

"Anything at all?" she asked, looking over her shoulder. "Do you mean that?"

"I do," he said, firmly. "I won't walk away. I'll see this through."

Liz turned and seemed to grow even less substantial, so that it became impossible to make out her expression in the glow of the laptop screen. She shimmered again, moved closer, and he stumbled back, holding up his hands as if they could ward her off. Her outline became blurred, and a cloud of grayness rolled over him, bringing a wave of intense cold. Then it was gone. He heard her voice, faint as if calling from a vast distance.

"Save me, Paul."

A tingling sensation ran around his wrists, his ankles, and pricked at his temples. A dreadful suspicion sprang up, and he rushed into the bathroom, flicked on the light above the mirror. As he had feared, the red marks around his wrists were deeper, raw indentations in the flesh. There was a shaving mirror mounted on a swivel stand next to the main mirror. He turned it until he could see the side of his head. A patch of red had appeared just above and behind his eyes. There was one on the other side.

Stigmata, he thought. *Marks of restraints, and where the electrodes were attached.*

"Are you inside me now?" he asked the mirror. "Have you decided to—to take up residence? To live through me?"

He waited for a response but heard none. He went back into the living room, started to email Mike Bryson, then gave up. There was nothing Mike could do. He was tired after the day's ordeal and resolved to try and get some sleep. He went to bed expecting nightmares. But, to his surprise, it seemed that only moments after his head hit the pillow, he was looking up at the ceiling, bright with an English summer dawn.

'Time to go, Paul.'

The voice was insistent, excited. A girl's voice. Paul sat up, swung his legs off the bed, decided to do without breakfast or shower. He had a task to perform. He had rested. Now came the challenge. He had made a promise and was expected to keep it.

'This is the end. I know it is. Don't be afraid.'

***

"You okay?" asked Kate. "Because frankly, you look terrible."

Paul looked at Rookwood's manager as if he did not recognize her. His hair was disheveled, he had not shaved, and he was wearing old sweats and sneakers that looked in need of a wash. Kate wrinkled her nose as he walked closer, stepped back. He smelled of stale sweat.

"We're fine," the American said, his voice expressionless. "We're just going outside for a moment. We won't be long."

Kate stared as Paul crossed the foyer to the main entrance, stopped. He stood for a moment, seeming to gather himself, as if he was preparing to leap through the open doorway. Then he took one step, gingerly putting his foot over the threshold. Suddenly Kate recalled Imelda Troubridge's behavior.

"Paul!" she shouted. "Is it Palmer?"

He did not respond. He lifted his other foot, swung it forward, seemed to become paralyzed. Then, like a man battling against some incredible force, he completed the second step. Kate started forward, then hesitated, afraid to risk intervening. Then she caught sight of Declan leaving his office and shouted for him.

"What's up?" the Irishman asked, running into the foyer, then caught sight of Paul. "Oh, Christ."

Paul was moving slowly, painfully, down the gravel driveway. Kate thought he almost looked like a mime walking against the wind. But there was nothing funny about it. Instead, she felt a sense of dread, wondering if this new development would herald more suffering, perhaps another death.

"What if he just walks into the road?" she asked Declan.

"We'll—I'll make sure he doesn't," replied the caretaker. "Maybe you should stay here. He might turn violent."

Kate watched as Declan walked briskly after Paul, feeling useless but unwilling to go after them. Her experiences the previous day had rattled her so badly she was thinking of leaving her job.

"Be careful, Dec!" she shouted, knowing it was a stupid thing to say.

Declan gave her a wave and a grin, then he was alongside Paul. The American showed no sign of noticing Declan and kept trudging painfully on toward the gate. The Irishman was talking to him now, but Kate could not hear what he was saying. Then Declan put out a hand, grasped Paul's arm.

A second later the caretaker was spinning wildly away from him, as if he was caught in a mini tornado. But there was no hint of wind. As Declan staggered and fell onto his backside, Paul continued to walk, slowly but without hesitation, towards gates of Rookwood.

Kate ran out to see if Declan was hurt. By the time she got to him he had already gotten up and was brushing his pants down.

"Well," he said ruefully, "I won't be touching that feller again. It was like being grabbed by a mad gorilla or something."

"An invisible gorilla."

Kate watched as Paul reached the open gate, stepped through on stiff legs, and vanished around the corner.

"Come on," she said. "We can at least watch out for him."

***

Liz was buried deep within his mind, a passenger of sorts. But whatever confined the ghosts to Rookwood could not be tricked. As soon as he stepped into the foyer, Paul felt something pulling him away, toward the East Wing. With each step he took, the influence became stronger, and he had to focus all his efforts on simply putting one foot in front of the other. He was only vaguely aware of his surroundings as a throbbing pain started to develop behind his eyes. The marks of electrodes and shackles grew more inflamed. Pain spread from the stigmata of Palmer's brutal experiments, and soon his whole body was in agony.

He heard a voice he recognized, felt someone touch his arm. Then the touch was gone. The throbbing pain behind his eyes evolved into a terrible migraine that impaired his vision. The sunlit lawns around him turned into a hellscape of lurid colors and blurred shapes. A noise like a surging ocean roared through his head. He reached the gates, stepped out onto the sidewalk.

'She has to be here. I know she is.'

Paul could not make sense of the words. He only knew that he had to keep going. He had given his word, he had promised to help. But the pain was submerging him, erasing all sense of self, burning away his good intentions, undermining his will power.

I can't go on! This will kill me. I have to go back.

Another voice now, one whose words he could not understand. It was a kindly voice, one that he thought he knew. Again, someone touched his arm. This time the hand was not snatched away. Instead, the contact brought a sudden lessening of pain, and Paul gasped in relief.

"I said, are you all right?"

His vision cleared enough for a round, worried face to become discernible. It was the gray-haired woman, looking up with concern in her eyes. It had not struck him before, but now Paul thought she looked kind, gentle. He felt a surge of emotion, so powerful he felt dizzy and staggered back against the wall of Rookwood.

"My baby."

The words left his mouth, but he had not spoken them. The woman looked startled, pulled her hand away. Paul tried to say something, apologize, explain, but he had lost control of his body.

"Oh, my baby!" he heard himself shout as he fell to his knees, sprawled on all fours. "My baby."

Emotion overwhelmed him, a sense of loss so great he began to sob uncontrollably. Paul knew he could not bear the feeling for long, that it would destroy him. There was a sudden spike of pain, blinding in its intensity, and then all discomfort was gone.

"What is it? What's wrong?"

The woman was staring down at him, puzzled and a little afraid. Then, her eyes widened, she put a hand to her mouth. Paul felt Liz, no longer a cold presence within him, but warm and shining like a miniature sun. The bright energy flowed out of him, played around the woman for a moment like a golden aurora, and then vanished.

Tears were streaming down the woman's face. Paul felt exhausted, shaken, but the only discomfort he felt was from the rough paving slabs under him. He tried to get up, realized he was drained, weak, and had to support himself against the wall.

"Did you—did you feel her?" he asked. "Did you sense her in some way?"

The woman nodded, her bottom lip quivering with emotion.

"I dreamed about this place," she stammered. "But I never dared go in. Every time I started to walk toward the gate something told me I had to turn back. Now I know why."

Paul nodded, still catching his breath.

"She didn't want you to be hurt," he said. "A good mother always tries to protect her child."

CHAPTER 11

"It was finally meeting her daughter," Paul explained. "Knowing that the one person she had ever truly loved was still alive and well. That was what freed her. Apparently, Sharon had been living down south for years, but she felt compelled to come back here. She was drawn to Rookwood but didn't know why."

Kate looked over to where Declan was giving a mug of hot, sweet tea to the gray-haired woman. Annie Semple's daughter had only said a few words since the bizarre encounter by the gates. She seemed to be suffering from mild shock, which was not surprising. But, like Paul, she seemed to have sustained no serious harm from the incident.

"Sharon's connection to Liz, or Annie, that was what freed her—her spirit, psyche, whatever you call it?" Kate asked.

Paul nodded.

"I guess so. Liz knew at some level that her daughter was the key to her freedom, even if she couldn't quite grasp it or articulate the truth. Do ghosts have subconscious motives? Anyway, it was the love she had felt for Sharon, the desperate need to see her again, that drove Liz. It freed her from this place."

Kate mulled that over for a few moments.

"Do you think something—well, similar, might get rid of the others? Some connection with the world beyond this place?"

Paul shook his head.

"I can't see love counting for anything with a callous son of a bitch like Palmer. Power, control, fame, they were all he ever wanted."

Kate shook her head in despair.

"Then we've not really moved on, have we?"

Paul shrugged.

"Put it this way," he said. "I'm moving out as soon as possible. With Liz gone, there's nothing to hold Palmer back."

***

"He might have been wrong. It's been very quiet."

Declan and Kate were standing at the furthermost end of the East Wing. It was almost three days since Paul Mahan had moved out. In that time, however, nothing unusual had happened. Kate had reconsidered her resignation and stopped applying for other positions.

Declan had gradually become less nervous. Now they were considering hiring a firm to finish the job of refurbishment, something that would have been unthinkable mere days ago.

"Fingers crossed," Kate replied. "The big boss has been on at me, asking when we can start advertising apartments again. I keep dodging the question."

"What about that scientist bloke?" asked Declan. "Is he still interested?"

"Another problem," Kate admitted. "I don't trust him—but he's very persistent. My real concern is that he'll stir things up again."

Seeing Declan's puzzlement, she went on.

"See, I've got my own theory—maybe things have stabilized. Maybe the conflict between Liz and Palmer was powering the whole haunting. Without that clash, the energy isn't there."

Declan felt dubious but did not disagree.

Just so long as I don't get waylaid by any more phantom gunmen, he thought.

They walked back through the East Wing, discussing the best way to progress work and keep the head office happy. Their footsteps echoed through empty rooms and hallways. As they reached the door leading into the main block Declan looked up. He could still make out the message that had been scrawled in blood. He had hastily covered the words with a layer of matt emulsion.

Note to self, paint over it again.

"Okay," said Kate, as they reached his office. "As it's the weekend, I get to knock off early and leave Rookwood to your tender mercies. If anything comes up, I'll be kicking back with my very good friend Pinot Grigio."

"Don't worry, you have a good one," Declan said.

Kate was almost out of the building when the screaming began.

***

Sadie Prescott filled the kettle for her midday cup of Assam tea. It was one of many rituals that gave form to her life. Today was Saturday, therefore she would read another two chapters of a not-too-literary novel, do her laundry, and clean the apartment.

While she waited for the water to boil, she dusted the photographs that adorned her fine Edwardian sideboard. As always, she murmured a little prayer for those relatives who had passed on. But this particular Saturday, she paused, feather duster in hand, and stared at one photograph in particular.

It was an old black and white picture of Sadie and her father on holiday in Brighton. Sadie had been twelve, her father a handsome forty-five. It was an image Sadie preferred to the way her dad had been at the end; unable to recognize anyone, an empty shell that barely resembled the strong, clever man she had worshipped.

"But that doesn't excuse what you did."

The voice was her father's, strong, authoritative. Sadie looked around the room, saw no one. For a moment she wondered if she had somehow heard a television set turned up far too loud, or one side of a conversation outside in the corridor. But the voice came again, and this time she was in no doubt the speaker was close by.

"My little girl, my little Sadie Sunshine. How could you do that to me?"

Only her father had called her Sadie Sunshine. Sobbing in fear and confusion, she covered her ears. But the voice was just as loud.

"It was murder. You picked up the pillow, held it right over my face, pushed down just hard enough."

"I couldn't stand it any longer!" she cried, running out into the kitchen, needing to do something and hoping to flee from the voice. "It was too much to bear! He was dead inside, he wasn't the man we'd all known. It was what he would have wanted!"

"My little Sadie Sunshine."

The voice was gloating, cruel. Sadie let her hands fall to her sides as the voice continued its litany of accusations.

"You are so selfish, cruel. A hypocrite, posing as a good woman, a believer, but always hiding a rotten heart, a corrupted soul. You don't deserve to live out your life content, secure, in peace."

Her father's face appeared in the cloud of steam issuing from the spout of the kettle. It was angry, contemptuous, judging and condemning her. Sadie's little kitchen suddenly seemed darker, and oddly crowded, as if it had suddenly filled with an unseen throng of people. The invisible crowd seemed to merge, condense into a single shadowy form that walked toward her, two brief glimmers of light where its eyes might be.

"No!" she gasped.

"Oh, but yes."

Sadie felt the darkness move inside her, take possession of her body, drive the battered remnants of her mind into a corner, stripping it of power. She was a spectator now, silently screaming as she felt her arm move, raising itself, reaching out. She saw her hand pick up the kettle, watched her arm raise it until the spout was level with her face.

***

"It was a message," Paul insisted, trying to keep his temper. "It was Palmer telling us all that he's still in business, that Rookwood is still his domain."

"Nonsense," retorted Rodria. "A mentally unstable woman committed an act of self-harm. It might not even be connected with the so-called haunting."

The two were arguing in the foyer of Rookwood. Since Sadie Prescott had been horribly disfigured, the apartment building had emptied of its remaining tenants. Lawsuits had been threatened, compensation demanded, rent withheld. The publicity had been devastating for the company. Kate's employers had ordered her to co-operate with Rodria, despite her reservations.

"You've no right to call Sadie mentally unstable," Paul protested. "She was as sane as me."

"With all due respect," Rodria said, his voice dripping with condescension, "the woman believed in spiritualism. And your belief that you've been in touch with the ghost of a dead girl doesn't say much for your mental state."

Declan grabbed Paul as he started toward Rodria.

"No punch ups, now," said the Irishman. "Let's keep this debate nice and intellectual, shall we?"

Paul tried to shake off Declan, but then felt ashamed. There was no way that an ego as big as Rodria's would be deflected from the chance to get some publicity. The university authorities weren't averse to it either, as Paul had found when he tried to block Rodria's plans.

"At least leave him to it," he said, turning to Kate. "Don't risk staying behind here."

"I've got no choice," the manager said. "Whatever I may think of this—this experiment, I'm required to supervise it."

Paul looked at Declan. It was clear from the caretaker's expression that he would not leave Kate. Paul smiled wryly and looked out of the foyer windows. A clump of reporters was gathered near the gates. Even they, it seemed, had gotten the message about Rookwood. Which made Rodria's confidence all the more infuriating.

"Max," Paul said, determined to make one final attempt. "A scientist is always skeptical, even of his own theories. What if you're wrong?"

Rodria did not even bother to reply, instead he turned to Kate to explain what was required of her and her staff. When Kate asked for details on exactly what Rodria intended, he answered with a flood of technical language.

"Delousing?" interrupted Declan, with an innocent face. "We're not dealing with fleas."

"Degaussing," snapped Max Rodria. "The process is sometimes called degaussing."

The scientist seemed to have taken an instant dislike to the caretaker, and the feeling seemed to be mutual. Paul wondered if he could exploit this in some way, but couldn't see how. Meanwhile, Rodria was delivering an impromptu lecture.

"The process was used during wartime to make ships less vulnerable to magnetic mines. Of course, we have refined it considerably, but the principle remains the same. A powerful electromagnetic field will neutralize any similar field in the fabric of the building. It's simply a case of reversing the polarity."

He broke off when a petite young woman in red-rimmed glasses appeared. Rodria's assistant was a small, meek-looking grad student, who seemed in awe of the scientist. She reminded Paul of Liz, in that she seemed far too young for adult responsibilities.

"Ah, Chris–the caretaker here will help unload the equipment. Won't he, Miss Bewick?"

Declan looked as if he might tell Rodria where to go, but after Kate gave him a pleading look, he went outside. The degausser wheeled into the foyer from the rented van looked impressive. It consisted of a large, roughly cubic mass of metal and plastic with a set of controls on one side.

The device was accompanied by a small gasoline generator. As Rodria explained, the regular electricity supply would not be reliable during what he termed 'the process'. Paul watched, still racking his brains for a way to stop the experiment, as Rodria supervised the placement of the equipment. He had chosen the room where Paul had first encountered Palmer, and where Liz had tried to scare off Imelda Troubridge.

"The East Wing is the focus of the phenomena," Rodria explained pompously, filming himself on a small camera, "therefore, we will fire up the device there."

"Has this—degaussing thing—has it ever actually worked?" asked Kate timidly, aware that her bosses might see the video.

"It has achieved very promising results in tests," Rodria responded.

"Lab tests, would those be?" asked Paul. "As in, not actual field tests in haunted buildings?"

Rodria did not deign to answer and turned to the degausser, barking out orders. Between them, Chris and Declan connected the generator cables. Then Rodria, with a pretentiously detailed running commentary, set a timer on the device.

"You don't have to stay, Paul," Kate pointed out quietly as they looked on. "You've officially moved out."

"Yeah, but I still feel responsible, somehow," Paul said. "This place should be torn down, not demagnetized or whatever. Nobody should live here until someone a lot smarter than Max over there figures out how to cleanse it."

Perversely, Paul found himself wishing Palmer would manifest himself in a way that even Rodria could not deny. But nothing had happened since Sadie Prescott had horrifically scalded herself. Paul could not help but think that Palmer was playing some demented game of his own, toying with everyone.

But what's his purpose? Paul wondered. *Even a madman has some kind of objective.*

"Right, let's start her up," ordered Rodria, making no move to help.

Chris struggled with the generator for a few moments before Declan, smiling politely, stepped in and got it running. The motor was shockingly loud in the confined space. Rodria, now shouting his running commentary over the generator, moved to the controls of the degausser. Paul made one more effort to persuade the scientist.

"Okay, Max, maybe there is some kind of energy field in the building, confining Palmer, or what Palmer has become. But these ghosts are not recordings. They're not insensate images or emotions being replayed. They are capable of thinking, adapting. You're making a big mistake."

The reply was predictable.

"A lot of medieval nonsense—there are no such things as ghosts!"

Rodria waved Paul aside and flicked a couple of switches, then pushed a green button. There was a slight hum, a low vibration that Paul felt as much as heard.

"Now, we leave," said Rodria. "When dealing with high voltages, better safe than sorry."

That's the first sensible thing you've said, Paul thought.

They filed out through one of the East Wing's doors, with Declan fastening the plastic sheet closed behind them. A minute later they had joined the small crowd of reporters and general gawkers at the gates. Rodria explained that the timer had been set for ten minutes, and passed the time giving the media an account of his accomplishments.

"Do you think this will work?" Paul asked Chris.

The young woman looked startled, and Paul wondered if she was unused to being asked her opinion.

"I'm sure it will," she replied. "You should show more respect to the professor. He's doing great work, demystifying the paranormal."

Hero worship, Paul thought cynically. But he persisted in asking Chris details about the degausser while the minutes ticked away. Eventually, the moment came, and Rodria announced grandly that 'the process is now complete.'

The scientist led a small column of reporters back up to Rookwood, accompanied by Kate and Declan. Chris and Paul tagged along behind, the meek assistant apparently under orders to stay in the background.

"He doesn't want you to get between him and the media, huh?" asked Paul.

The young woman did not reply. Rodria led his posse into the East Wing, and the group gathered around the bulk of the degausser. The scientist launched into a basic explanation of what had happened—according to himself, at least. Paul grew frustrated as reporters lobbed softball questions, and Rodria claimed that 'any so-called haunting has probably been neutralized.'

"How can you know?" Paul shouted from the back.

Rodria sneered.

"One of my esteemed colleagues, there, who moved out of the building to escape the bogies," he said.

"But seriously," one journalist asked, "how can you know things have returned to normal, whatever that is?"

Rodria puffed himself up like a bullfrog and resumed his diatribe. However, he broke off after a few seconds because he was clearly losing his audience.

"Oh my God!" exclaimed Kate. "It hasn't worked."

Paul could not see what was happening at first. But then a couple of reporters blocking his view stepped back, collided with him, and pushed past. Paul could see what had spooked them now. Behind Rodria there were too many shadows, and they were moving slowly, hypnotically. The swirl of dark shapes grew more substantial. There was a general movement back, toward the exit to the grounds.

A sudden wave of cold penetrated through Paul's clothes. Other people noticed it, too, and more people moved toward the door.

"What's wrong?" Rodria demanded. His breath was visible, a rapidly dispersing cloud in front of his face. Then he turned, peered at the gathering darkness. A vibration began to throb through the floor and walls, a blizzard of plaster fell from the ceiling. Almost everyone was either outside or leaving in confusion that bordered on panic. Paul began to back off, taking Chris by the arm, pulling her away.

"This is not happening!" Rodria bellowed. "This is not acceptable!"

Rodria, Paul realized, was offended that the ghosts had not stuck to the script. This was not meant to happen. The shadowy presence flowed like vapor toward Rodria, then seemed to hesitate. As the scientist stood, apparently refusing to accept the evidence of his own senses, the darkness surrounded the generator and Rodria's magnetic device. The cold was intense, almost Arctic.

"Get out!" Paul shouted. "Run!"

Just before he fled Paul saw the dark presence coalesce into a human figure—short, narrow-shouldered, with gleaming circles for eyes. Miles Rugeley Palmer glared up at Max Rodria, who had finally fallen silent. Then another shockwave ran through the building, and Paul retreated. The familiar plastic sheet fell back to cover the door. Through it, Paul could just make out vague shapes moving. One, he assumed, was Rodria.

"We must help him!"

Chris, the scientist's assistant, was looking up at Paul, her expression pleading. Paul was about to warn her not to risk going back inside when there was a crackling sound. The plastic was pushed aside, and Max Rodria emerged into the July sunlight. He looked disheveled, his face pale, but he seemed unharmed.

"Max!" Chris cried, and ran over to her boss.

Rodria looked down at her with a blank expression, then smiled benignly.

"Ah, my dear girl, there's nothing to worry about," he said. "As I predicted, whatever traces of past events that lingered in the building—"

Rodria stopped, his expression changing. He looked confused, then seemed to catch sight of Paul.

"You!" he bellowed. "You always tried to undermine me, denigrate my work, hold me up to ridicule!"

Rodria strode toward Paul, almost knocking Chris down in his fury, and with him, came the now familiar wave of unnatural cold. Paul retreated, stumbled, fell on the uneven turf. Around him he saw people gawping, the cameraman filming, but nobody moving to intervene. Rodria descended upon Paul, who was struggling to stand up. The scientist kicked at Paul's leg, sending him sprawling, then kicked again, the toe of his brown brogue connecting with a rib.

"Hey, that's out of order mate!"

Declan ran at Rodria and grappled with the older man. Paul, winded and unable to move, assumed the Irishman would easily subdue the seemingly insane professor. But Rodria flung Declan aside, as if the older man had suddenly acquired superhuman strength. In that moment, he knew what was happening.

Rodria started forward again, walking quickly toward the gates. People stood aside as the scientist barged through the small crowd, ignoring questions from reporters.

"Stop him!" Paul managed to shout. "Don't let them escape."

As he got to his feet, he pointed at Rodria's back, tried to find the right words.

"He's possessed! Palmer's using him to escape."

Declan looked at Paul, wide-eyed, then seemed to make a decision. He ran at Rodria, tackled him, and brought the hefty man down. Again, Rodria began kicking out, but now Paul and Kate had joined Declan. Among them, they managed to restrain him. Rodria glared at Paul, spat in his face, kept trying to break free.

"Get him back inside," Paul urged. "It could kill him if this goes on too long."

"You meddling bastard!" snarled Rodria. "You can't defeat us. Let us go free!"

As they dragged the big man back to the East Wing, the cursing became more inventive, profoundly obscene. Rodria's voice also shifted in tone, becoming thinner, higher, as Palmer came to the fore.

They were too good a match, thought Paul, as they half-dragged the scientist over the grass. *Palmer's ego must have meshed with Rodria's almost perfectly.*

Once more inside the building, Rodria suddenly became limp. They almost dropped him. The cold was even more intense now they were indoors. Paul felt a sudden nausea, felt a tingling like a static charge run over his skin.

But it was too late. With a loud snap, the thick, black generator cables broke free from the degausser and lashed out at Rodria. The tips of the metallic tentacles crackled, dropped sparks. When they struck Rodria, there was a blinding flash. The scientist jerked, writhing on the tiled floor, and the cables wrapped around him as smoke rose from a huge burn mark on his tweed jacket.

With a piercing scream, Chris ran for the exit, followed by Paul. Outside, the well-kept lawns of Rookwood were dotted with pale-faced witnesses. One cameraman from a local TV news service was checking his equipment, hands clumsy with shock. Chris was gazing at the outer doorway to the East Wing, face contorted with horror.

"What happened?"

It was the reporter from the *Tynecastle Gazette*, looking at Paul as if he had some special insight to offer.

"He got himself killed," he said simply.

"But what happened, and why?" the woman persisted.

Paul shook his head, turned to look back at the East Wing. Bright sparks were visible through the door and windows. The electrical equipment was still malfunctioning. He wondered if Rodria's experiment had actually boosted the energy available to the entity Palmer had become.

And now Max is subject to Palmer's deranged whims.

He had to laugh, albeit grimly, at the thought of Rodria's massive ego being enslaved by anyone, even a long-dead maniac. In fact, the more he thought about it, the more he wondered if some great clash of wills was currently underway in the East Wing of Rookwood.

"It's on fire!" someone shouted.

They were right. Paul could see smoke emerging from the East Wing, and the flashes of electric sparks had been replaced by the orange glow of flames.

He remembered the fuel tank of Rodria's generator and heard sirens growing closer.

EPILOGUE

"And you haven't heard anything more from—from Liz?"

Paul shook his head, continued to gaze up at a picture on the wall above the woman's head.

"So far as I know she's moved on to heaven, or the astral plane, or maybe Nirvana."

Doctor Weller shifted in her seat, wrote a few words on her pad. Paul felt, not for the first time, a deep desire to read her notes.

I could always ask, he thought. *But that might not be appropriate.*

"You appreciate that this is not the kind of thing I normally hear," she said. "At least, not in cases of depression."

"I've told you what occurred," Paul pointed out. "Crazy or not, it's what happened to me. And I've filled in a few details from what other people said."

The doctor made another note.

"Is there anything particularly interesting about that picture?" she asked, twisting round to look at the painting.

Paul looked at the doctor, shrugged. The painting was a reproduction of a dull seascape, with a little sailboat on a calm ocean, under a blue sky with a few fleecy white clouds.

"I just find it helpful to focus on something—relaxing, while I'm talking about all this," he admitted. "I suppose you choose pictures for that reason?"

"Well, we're not going to put Hieronymus Bosch up there," she smiled. "Nothing that might cause agitation or be too distracting. Now, perhaps it would help if you told me more about your mother..."

The session continued, with Paul gradually peeling back layers of memory, revealing things he had never told anyone before. He felt it was probably helping and told Doctor Weller so. But there was one thing he could not reveal. It was, he suspected, a legacy from his close contact with Liz, coupled with the more general ordeal he had undergone at Rookwood. It was an intermittent problem, but just at the moment, it seemed to be manifesting itself with some intensity.

"Did this place used to be a children's home?" he asked suddenly.

The therapist stopped in mid-remark, surprised by the question. She looked speculatively at Paul for a moment, then made another note.

"Yes, I believe so," she replied. "Some kind of Victorian orphanage, anyhow. Why do you ask?"

"Oh, just something I—I read it somewhere, I guess," he said, trying to sound casual. "Sorry, please go on."

Paul made a determined effort to focus on the questions, give intelligent responses, be as truthful as he could. But he began to suspect that this was not going to work. It was not because Doctor Weller was unhelpful—far from it. It was because they were not alone.

No matter how intently he stared at the picture of the serene little boat, he could not ignore the shifting figures that were a little too substantial to be shadows. They stood behind the therapist, peering over her shoulder, jostling to see what she thought of Paul. They were small figures, and sometimes they became substantial enough for Paul to make out pale, thin faces, and their antiquated clothes. He thought of the high death rate infectious diseases used to inflict on the young, especially the poorest children. He felt pity for them, but also fear of what might happen if he spoke to them.

No, he thought, *I'd better not ask what she's written. It could cause more trouble than it's worth.*

***

"I'm just saying," said Neve's mother. "It's shocking the way things are, these days."

"Yes, mum," replied Neve. "Shocking."

She had learned a long time ago not to argue with her mother about the state of the nation.

"Finish your cereal, miss," she added, speaking to Ella. "You'll be late for school again, and we don't want more trouble there, do we?"

Ella remained sitting still, spoon paused above the bowl of cornflakes. She was obviously listening to the grownups, head cocked to one side. Neve's mother was still bustling around the cramped kitchen, despite Neve's insistence that she could manage.

Sooner we get a place of our own the better, Neve thought. *I'm going barmy living here. And it's not good for Ella, seeing us bickering.*

"I'm just saying," Mrs. Cotter repeated. "In my day, people had more respect. You could leave your front door unlocked because there wasn't all this crime going on."

At that, Ella tilted her head the other way, nodded. Neve was about to tell her off when the girl spoke.

"That's not true, granny," she said firmly, waving her spoon for emphasis. "In the old days there were lots of criminals around here, and people locked their doors at night."

Both women looked at Ella in startled silence. Neve tried not to laugh, seeing her mother's face.

"What are they teaching them these days?" said Mrs. Cotter finally. "How on earth would you know about that, missy?"

Ella shrugged and began to scoop up her cereal. Her grandmother made a disapproving noise but withdrew from the fray and went out to fuss in other rooms. Neve gulped down the last of her coffee and then started searching in her handbag for her keys.

"You put them in the bowl on the sideboard, mummy," said Ella. "Along with granny's keys."

"Oh, thanks," Neve replied, then stopped, stared. It was not like Ella to know where anything of her mother's was. Rather the opposite, in fact.

She's been acting quite oddly, Neve thought. *But that's not surprising, given what she's been through. We'll see what the child psychologist makes of it next week.*

"Darling," Neve said, sitting opposite her daughter. "We're very lucky to be able to live with granny, you know? Without her, we'd really be in a pickle. And we'll soon have a new place, a nice place."

Ella nodded.

"I won't say anything about the old days anymore," she promised.

Neve smiled, reached over to ruffle Ella's hair. Then she frowned, took hold of her daughter's free hand. Ella pulled away quickly, shoveled up another mouthful of cereal.

"Have you hurt yourself, poppet?" Neve asked anxiously, getting up. "Let me see."

"No," Ella insisted, not meeting her mother's eye. "It's all right. I'm fine."

For a moment, Neve thought about persisting, then saw the clock on the kitchen wall. They were going to be late, and the matter would wait. She had to get Ella out of the door and into the car, tackle the rush hour traffic, apologize to the teacher for yet another late start...

By the time she collected Ella from school that day, Neve had almost resolved to take her to a doctor. But she discreetly checked the girl's hands as they drove home and decided against it. Whatever had caused them, the faint red marks around Ella's wrists had disappeared.

* * *

If you enjoyed the book, please leave a review. Your reviews inspire us to continue writing about the world of spooky and untold horrors!

Check out these best-selling books from our talented authors

Ron Ripley (Ghost Stories)

- Berkley Street Series Books 1 – 9
  www.scarestreet.com/berkleyfullseries
- Moving in Series Box Set Books 1 – 6
  www.scarestreet.com/movinginboxfull

A. I. Nasser (Supernatural Suspense)

- Slaughter Series Books 1 – 3 Bonus Edition
  www.scarestreet.com/slaughterseries

David Longhorn (Sci-Fi Horror)

- Nightmare Series: Books 1 – 3
  www.scarestreet.com/nightmarebox
- Nightmare Series: Books 4 – 6
  www.scarestreet.com/nightmare4-6

Sara Clancy (Supernatural Suspense)

- Banshee Series Books 1 – 6
  www.scarestreet.com/banshee1-6

For a complete list of our new releases and best-selling horror books, visit www.scarestreet.com/books

See you in the shadows,
Team Scare Street

Made in the USA
Middletown, DE
05 April 2023